Unfortunately, there **vo**
things wro **..**
Matt wasn **d**
Taddeo was

She must have made a sound because suddenly both of them were looking at her. The expression of pleasure in their dark eyes was subtly different, but there were almost identical smiles of welcome on their faces.

'Lissa! You're late! Papa has already started the story,' Taddeo exclaimed. 'Come and sit next to me so you can see the pictures.'

When she hesitated Matt seconded the invitation.

'Yes, Lissa. Come and sit next to us so you can find out if the sky is really falling down.'

There was a sweet pain in leaning close to the two of them to share the book. One half of her mind was relishing every nuance, from the fresh, soapy smell of Taddeo's skin to the deep resonance of Matt's voice. The other half was desperately trying to preserve even a little distance, so that when she was no longer part of their circle her heart wouldn't forever mourn their loss.

Josie Metcalfe lives in Cornwall now, with her long-suffering husband, her four children having flown the nest, but, as an army brat frequently on the move, books became the only friends who came with her wherever she went. Now that she writes them herself she is making new friends, and hates saying goodbye at the end of a book—but there are always more characters in her head clamouring for attention until she can't wait to tell their stories.

Recent titles by the same author:

COMING HOME TO DANIEL
THREE LITTLE WORDS
TWO'S COMPANY
ONE AND ONLY

THE ITALIAN EFFECT

BY
JOSIE METCALFE

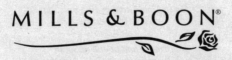

MILLS & BOON®

First published in Great Britain 2001
Harlequin Mills & Boon Limited,
Eton House, 18-24 Paradise Road, Richmond, Surrey TW9 1SR

© Josie Metcalfe 2001

ISBN 0 263 82691 0

Set in Times Roman 10½ on 12 pt.
03-1001-49549

Printed and bound in Spain
by Litografía Rosés, S.A., Barcelona

CHAPTER ONE

Two days into her holiday Lissa flopped back on her beach towel and heaved a great sigh.

She might have booked it at the very last minute, but it was all exactly as the travel agent had promised. The Italian sky was impossibly blue, the sand was soft and white and the sun was warm and bright.

It wasn't exactly the exotic Far-Eastern destination she'd been looking forward to for the last six months, but it was her grandmother's native country. She just wished she were visiting it under happier circumstances.

As it was, all around her was a complete selection of nationalities and every one of them, from the oldest to the youngest, was enjoying themselves…and she was already bored to tears.

'There's nothing to *do*,' she muttered, slapping shut the thick glitzy novel she'd picked up at the airport and closing her eyes in disgust. It was by a favourite author and she'd been so certain that it would be able to hold her attention. She *needed* it to be able to hold her attention because there were things she didn't want to have time to think about.

After the last year of non-stop activity and the excitement of making all those plans for her future… No, she wasn't going to think about *that* disaster and the way it had changed her life for ever.

She desperately needed this break and had been looking forward to having time to relax, but, oh, she was finding it so hard to unwind.

Yesterday she'd hired a car to take a preliminary look at the local sights and had promised herself a longer look at the nearby countryside which her grandmother had described so many times. She had a whole month to fill, after all, she reminded herself with a silent groan, and it was still far too soon to start thinking about anything further away than that.

This morning she'd even visited the hotel's beauty salon for more than an hour's pampering and then had promptly undone most of the beautician's efforts with a dip in the sea. Unless she was willing to waste her time wandering around the small parade of souvenir-filled shops lining the sea front, all that remained was to lie here and listen to the world go by.

Thank goodness the ice-cream vendor seemed to have switched his chimes off for a while. It had been a welcome surprise to recognise the very English sound of 'Greensleeves' instead of the ubiquitous 'O sole mio'— at least until the thirty-seventh repetition.

Lissa sighed again and then forced herself to play the game of trying to separate out all the different elements of the sounds surrounding her.

First and most pervasive was the rhythmic susurration of the waves on the shore, punctuated by the raucous shrieks of seabirds. She'd watched them earlier, wheeling about the edges of the rocky outcrops that edged the beach.

Almost as raucous were the children, their cries and laughter ebbing and flowing around her with the intermittent thuds of running feet. There were several family groups with youngsters ranging from a few months old to young teenagers, and the way they all seemed to play together it was difficult to tell which children belonged with which parents.

Nearby was a young couple, honeymooners by the self-obsessed look of them and the shiny newness of their matching wedding rings. Their soft murmurs reached her on the fitful breeze and faded every so often into meaningful silences and husky laughter.

If the steamy kiss she'd witnessed a few moments ago was anything to go by, it wouldn't be long before they disappeared back to their room. When it happened, she wouldn't allow herself to dwell on the fact that she was probably the only person on the beach by herself; that she should have been part of a pair by now, if only...

She shook her head to dispel the thought before it got any further and concentrated again on the life going on around her, determined to become part of it even if only by observation.

There was a group of young men farther over, fit and healthy and obviously proud of revealing it in their choice of skimpy beachwear. They were locals if their dark hair and deep tans were any indication and had been taking a delight in passing comments among themselves about the women going by. Apparently they were assuming that pale skin meant their targets were newly arrived visitors ripe for a holiday romance. They were also clearly taking it for granted that the women they were dissecting wouldn't understand their conversation.

It wasn't the first time that Lissa was glad of her own mixed heritage. Not only did her dark hair and the natural olive tint of her skin offer her a degree of protection against these predators, but her comprehension of Italian was easily good enough to put her on her guard. An insult spoken with an apparently admiring smile was still an insult.

She heard a group of giggling female English voices

arrive nearby and opened one eye to peer in their direction. It didn't take long to discover that they were apparently a group of girls on their first foreign holiday without their parents.

Lissa could remember that age of innocence—just left school and waiting for exam results to know whether she was going to be able to follow her dream of becoming a doctor—but it seemed so much longer than ten years ago.

She didn't need a crystal ball to know what was going to happen next and the grim inevitability of it kept her watching.

It only took a few minutes for the local males to close in on their new quarry with swaggering walks and gleaming smiles. The girls clearly didn't understand the crudity of the comments being made about them and their physical attributes, or the bargaining going on between the men as they apportioned the girls among themselves. Lissa could, and it turned her stomach to see them led off like lambs to the slaughter.

She closed her eyes again but what little pleasure she'd found in the day had been soured. It didn't seem to matter that she tried to concentrate on the soothing sounds of the ocean. All she seemed to hear were the insincere compliments that had been showered on the naïve girls just a few feet away. How long would it be before their eyes were opened? Hours? Days? At least it wouldn't be longer than the one- or two-week span of their holiday.

In her case, it had taken months for the penny to drop.

She tried to shut the sounds out and was seriously contemplating going back to the hotel when she heard a new sound added to the cacophony and every nerve switched to full alert.

'Oh, my God,' shrieked a voice not far away, a young and obviously frightened girl's voice. 'Help me, someone. He's fallen. He's hurt…'

Lissa was on her feet almost before she realised she was moving, her eyes scanning the far end of the beach.

Several other people had obviously heard the scream and they were all looking towards the rocks that curved round like a protective arm at the far end of the strip of sand.

Second nature had her reaching for her bag and then she was off and running.

A small crowd had started gathering, several voices calling out advice.

Lissa sent up a silent prayer of gratitude that she'd never lost her basic comprehension of Italian even though her speech might not be quite fluent. It was certainly enough to understand that the voices in the crowd were suggesting that the unseen victim should be moved into a more comfortable position.

'*Fermo! Non muoverti!*' she shouted as she pushed her way through the gathering knot of onlookers, terrified that they might move the victim and damage his spinal cord. '*Stia attento della spina dorsale!*'

Her voice must have conveyed both the urgency of the situation and the fact that she was an authority of some sort, because everyone stood back to let her through. Even the young woman who had first called the alarm grew silent, but tears still streamed down her face as an older woman wrapped her in comforting arms.

'*Chiami un'ambulanza!*' she ordered as soon as she caught sight of the scene in front of her, then dropped to her knees in the sand and concentrated on beginning her observations.

She couldn't help thinking that the little boy lying crumpled and unconscious on the unforgiving rocks looked just like an abandoned puppet. He looked so small and fragile that she just wanted to pick him up and cradle him in her arms.

'ABC,' she murmured under her breath, grounding herself in the routine she'd been following ever since she'd begun her training in emergency medicine. 'Airway, breathing, circulation.'

He was lying on his back across the rocks with his head twisted to one side, but all the while he was able to breathe it was far safer not to move his neck. His pulse was good, too…a little fast but strong and regular.

In between, she was being peppered with information about her little charge. It seemed as if almost half of the people on the beach knew little Taddeo.

A voice called something from the back of the rapidly growing crowd and the message was passed forward. With so many voices chiming in it could have been garbled, but Lissa understood enough. There had been an accident a few miles up the coast. A car had crashed into a motorcycle. It could take half an hour or even more before qualified help arrived.

'It's up to me, then,' she murmured as she rested her fingers gently over the steady pulse in the fragile neck. 'No proper equipment. Nothing except all those years of training to fall back on.'

Suddenly her brain seemed to be working at lightning speed.

'I need a small surfboard,' she announced, the Italian word emerging from her mouth without conscious thought. She'd been watching some of the children riding the waves into shore on them a little while ago and one of them would have to serve as a makeshift backboard. 'And some towels and some leather belts... Oh, and some strong men with gentle hands.'

'Wouldn't we all?' quipped one of the women in the crowd. There was a sudden ripple of laughter at her wry comment and Lissa couldn't help smiling, in spite of the tense situation.

It took very little time for her strange shopping list to arrive and then it was a case of demonstrating exactly what she needed her untrained assistants to do.

It seemed as if it took for ever before she had five-year-old Taddeo positioned to her satisfaction, his head braced by rolled-up towels on either side to prevent his neck from moving and held still by several strips of adhesive tape from the first-aid kit in her bag. The rest of his body was cushioned by more towels and stabilised by the borrowed belts wrapped around the board.

He was still unconscious and there was a large knot on the back of his head that was bleeding sluggishly. It didn't look as if he'd broken any limbs, but only an X-ray would tell. As for any further injuries...

'Carry him carefully,' she encouraged the men who took either end of the board. 'Don't slip or you'll jolt him. We don't want to risk paralysing him.'

She raced back across the narrow beach to grab the rest of her belongings before rejoining the small cavalcade, sparing a brief reassuring smile for the young woman being comforted by the matriarch of the boisterous family.

It was a precarious trek up the winding pathway to the road at the top. She'd taken the much steeper steps on the way down, but even this route seemed almost as precipitous as Mount Everest now that she wanted to cover the distance quickly.

She knew that the first hour after an accident—the

so-called 'golden' hour—could be the most crucial in deciding the survival of a patient. It would have been impossible not to be conscious that time was ticking by at an alarming rate.

'*La macchina,*' announced one of the volunteer porters as they came to a halt beside a luxurious car.

While she supervised the loading of her little charge across the back seat she subdued a brief pang of worry at abandoning her own hired vehicle. It could be awkward if she was left stranded at the hospital without transport, but it was far more important that she should be close at hand to watch over Taddeo.

Lissa perched herself on the edge of the seat, bracing her hip against the edge of the makeshift backboard to ensure it didn't shift as the engine roared into life. She tightened one hand over the luxurious leather upholstery, the other probing gently around the wedged towels to check on her charge's pulse.

Still strong and steady, thank goodness, although his continued unconsciousness was worrying. Supposing he had sustained something more than concussion? A haemorrhage? Brain damage? Was he in a coma, dying even as she counted his pulse and monitored his breathing?

'Don't be stupid,' she muttered, giving herself a mental shake. 'Just because you aren't surrounded by the usual equipment in the emergency department doesn't mean that your brain isn't functioning the way it usually does.' She checked the size of the child's pupils, having to peer closely because the irises were so dark a brown that they almost merged with the pupil.

'Still even,' she whispered, relieved that they also seemed to be equally responsive to changes in light levels.

'*Uno minuto,*' her unofficial ambulance driver called over his shoulder, announcing their imminent arrival at the hospital. Lissa sighed with relief, then started to brace herself for the task of dredging up enough of her rusty Italian to try to explain the situation and her observations.

She marshalled her thoughts into some semblance of order and spared a brief thought for the paramedics who had to do this on a daily basis. She'd always appreciated the ones who managed to give the maximum of pertinent detail in the minimum of words but had never realised how difficult it could be to do it.

'*Può aiutarmi?*' she called, beckoning two gentlemen in uniform standing near the entrance to the small regional hospital's emergency entrance. They certainly looked strong enough to help to lift the makeshift stretcher out of the car.

'There's been an accident. He's hit his head. He's unconscious,' she said, relieved that the hastily collected phrases had the desired effect.

Her redundant driver waved off her expressions of gratitude and called his good wishes after her as she hurried away. In no time at all she was following the child into the department, relieved to have arrived so swiftly.

Once inside the doors she was stopped by a wall of bodies and sound, unable to believe her eyes.

The whole place seemed to be completely crowded with a multitude of people wailing in misery, and for a moment she wondered how on earth she was going to get her little charge the attention he urgently needed.

Her press-ganged porters obviously knew their way around, as there was no hesitation in their passage through the unit. She followed closely behind, her eyes darting around in the hopes of spotting someone in authority as soon as possible.

One of her willing companions called out urgently to a harried nurse who pointed towards a curtained cubicle. The woman's reply was totally incomprehensible to Lissa, the words lost in the volume of misery surrounding them.

Lissa supervised as they gently deposited their burden onto an examining table then checked the little figure again. There was still no sign that he was returning to consciousness and she was growing increasingly frustrated that there was absolutely nothing she could do about the delay in getting someone to look at him.

If this had been the accident and emergency department she'd been working in for the last year, she wouldn't even have had to raise her voice to have at least a nurse in attendance. What kind of place was this to have the reception area filled with such a noisy rabble and not a member of medical staff in evidence? Was there *anyone* in charge?

When the curtain was whisked aside behind her she whirled to face the intruder. She would have loved to demand answers to each one of those questions but doubted whether her grasp of Italian was up to it. Neither was it the time or place for such recriminations. It was Taddeo who mattered.

A distant part of her brain registered the fact that the man who had just joined them was the epitome of every cliché about handsome Italian males—all lean good looks and flashing dark eyes. The more rational side registered the fact that his clothing might be in immaculate good taste but it was decidedly rumpled and he looked as exhausted as if he hadn't slept for a week.

That didn't mean that those dark eyes were lazy about

skimming over her from head to toe, lingering pointedly in several places.

Lissa glared at him when his gaze finally rose high enough to reach her face, angry that her body was stirring in response to the admiration she could read there.

The sudden shiver of awareness drew her attention to the fact that she was wearing little more than a gauzy shirt over a swimsuit that covered her as faithfully as a second skin. It was a measure of how single-minded her concentration had been over the last half-hour that she'd completely forgotten her skimpy attire, but now wasn't the time to dwell on it.

'You are a doctor?' she demanded with a lift of her chin that denied the previous few seconds of byplay, and received a cool nod in reply. 'Well, there's been an accident,' she announced, the words beginning to sound more fluent the more often she used them. 'The child fell and hit his head. He's still unconscious.' She gestured towards her charge, affording him his first view of their patient.

He gasped and she found herself unceremoniously nudged aside as he strode to the side of the bed.

'*Mio figlio!*' he exclaimed in a voice full of horror as he began to examine the child, and they were almost the only words she understood in the following flood of words. All she could tell was that they were questions and that he was very angry.

'I'm sorry, but when you speak so fast I can't understand,' she announced, reverting to English and stopping him in his tracks. 'Did you say he's your son?'

'*Si...* Yes,' he corrected himself impatiently, his dark brows pulled together in a deep V as he checked the unconscious child's pupillary reaction. 'Taddeo Aldarini. He's almost five years old... But what happened to him? Where is Maddelena, and what are *you* doing with my son?'

He'd straightened up by then and his final question was almost an accusation, not softened at all by the sexy accent shaping his words.

Lissa chose to answer the more important one first.

'He fell at the beach and landed on his back on the rocks.' She held up her hand when he went to interrupt. 'He's been unconscious since he fell but his vital signs are all within normal bounds. I didn't let anyone move him until I could stabilise his spine on an improvised backboard. As far as I can see, his only external injury is a bump on the back of his head where the skin has been broken.'

'You are a nurse?' he questioned as he swiftly jotted down what she'd told him on the case notes.

'A doctor,' she corrected as an amplified voice cut through the hubbub outside the curtain. The electronic distortion meant that she understood little more than the fact that the man was being paged in a hurry.

'What sort of a doctor?' he demanded with a suspicious look.

'Accident and emergency for the last year but I've been thinking about going into general practice.' At least, she had been before her private life had collapsed in ruins around her.

'You can prove this?' he challenged with a harried look over his shoulder as the disembodied voice called his name again.

'Now? No,' she said, startled by the demand. Was he going to sue her for practising medicine without permission in a foreign country? But Italy was part of the European Union. Didn't that mean that people were free to work in any of the member states?

The thoughts scrambling around in her head screeched to a halt with the memory of her little bag of belongings.

'Just a minute.' She crouched down to tip everything out onto the floor and grabbed the flat leather wallet hidden right at the bottom. 'Is this what you want to see?'

She held out both her passport and her hospital identity card. She had no idea how she'd come to pack it when she'd had no intention of doing anything other than vegetate for the next four weeks, but when she'd been preparing for her day on the beach had found it with the rest of her documents.

He examined both of them in silence then gave a decisive nod.

'I would like to ask a favour of you,' he said, his choice of words strangely formal. 'Would you accompany Taddeo to the...*radiografia*? As you see, I already have so many people waiting and now there are the victims of...*scontrarsi*.' He mimed a collision and gestured towards the throng all too audible on the other side of the curtain, but his glance towards his son was very telling. He was obviously torn between his duty to his patients and his personal wish to be beside his son.

Strictly speaking, it wasn't her problem but, having become involved in the situation, how could she *not* see it through?

'I'll stay with him on one condition—that you find me something a little more...' She gestured towards her skimpy attire with a grimace. It had seemed fairly modest on the beach, but next to his fully clothed body, there was something almost...intimate about the contrast.

'It would be a shame to hide such beauty,' he said

in a low voice and she glimpsed a sudden unnerving flash of heat in his dark eyes. 'But perhaps it would be safer.'

An hour later, Lissa's pulse still tended to miss a beat when she thought about the startling potency of that glance. The only way she'd been able keep it under some sort of control was to concentrate on her little charge.

It had been a major undertaking to dredge up enough Italian to make herself understood, especially as those long conversations with her grandmother had never covered such topics as 'make sure you leave the towels in position around his head until you've taken the X-ray of his neck'.

Along the way, she found several members of staff who spoke good English—better than her Italian, at any rate—and was able to ask some tactful questions. By the time she'd collected the evidence that Taddeo had suffered no broken or cracked bones, she'd also started to build up a picture of why the accident and emergency department was in such chaos.

'Dr Aldarini, would you like to set your mind at rest?' she invited when she finally managed to track him down with the developed X-ray plates.

He pounced on them so eagerly that Lissa was glad that she'd thought to bring them down to him. It was obvious that he'd been worrying about his son in spite of the fact that he was still rushed off his feet.

While he scrutinised each plate minutely, she did the same to him, wondering just what it was about this man, rumpled and exhausted as he was, that set up this strange electric tingle inside her. She couldn't remember having had anything quite like it happen to her before and it was totally inappropriate. Not only was she in

Italy for rest and recuperation in the wake of the disaster of the last few months, but this man was obviously a pillar of the local community. He was probably a very loving husband to the pretty young wife she'd had to leave behind at the beach and he was definitely a concerned parent.

She made herself drag her eyes away from him to gauge how many patients there were still waiting for attention.

None seemed to be victims of the outbreak of food-poisoning she'd heard about. Apparently, there had been some sort of welcoming buffet at one of the larger hotels a little way along the coast, resulting in nearly fifty people suffering the effects of the flouting of hygiene regulations in the kitchen.

'Where is Taddeo now?' Dr Aldarini demanded when he finished scrutinising the plates, and she turned to face him again. 'Is he on his way back down here?'

'I hope you don't think I was throwing my weight around, but...he came round while the X-rays were being taken and the radiographer and I decided he would probably be better off under supervision in the children's ward. Apparently the paediatrician already knows him there?'

His mouth twisted into a wry grin. 'Unfortunately, too well,' he agreed. 'The last time he was here was several months ago when he came off his *bicicletta* and broke his arm.' He shook his head. 'He has no fear, that one. He will give me white hair.'

Her eyes travelled over the thick dark strands but couldn't see any evidence that it was happening yet. All she noticed was the fact that his hair was just long enough to reveal the same existence of a tendency to unruly curls as his son had inherited.

'The paediatrician said that as he'd been unconscious for so long, he'll keep Taddeo here overnight under observation. He'll speak to you when you have time to call, but he was cautiously optimistic…the way doctors always are. Oh, and I have no idea how you'll get in contact with your wife to let her know what's happening. She was very upset, but I had to leave her behind at the beach. You'll need to put her mind at rest about Taddeo.'

She couldn't help thinking that the young woman she'd left at the beach seemed absurdly young to be married to such a man as this—still dynamic in spite of his exhaustion. And it wasn't just because he'd made her pulse leap when she'd been determined not to have anything to do with men for the foreseeable future.

'Taddeo has no mother,' he announced bluntly, his voice as hard as stone for all his attractive accent. 'Maddelena is the daughter of a colleague.'

Now, why on earth should his brusque words send a shaft of pleasure through her? she thought crossly. Why should it matter that the man wasn't married? For all she knew, he might be involved in a relationship with Maddelena, although his tone of voice didn't make it sound likely.

Anyway, it was none of her business. Her fleeting connection with the man would be over as soon as she found some way of returning to her hotel.

'Do you have a car, or may I give you a lift somewhere?' he asked suddenly, almost as if he'd been reading her mind. 'I will be free as soon as I've visited my son.'

She hesitated, torn between the strange feeling that she should get as far away from this man as possible and the equally strong desire to spend just a little longer in his company. In the end, practicality tipped the balance.

'I would be grateful for a lift,' she replied, equally politely. 'I travelled here with Taddeo, so my car is miles away.'

'After your actions today, it is the least I can do,' he said sincerely and gestured towards the bank of lifts. She found herself automatically falling into step beside him as he made his way towards the paediatric department.

Taddeo was almost asleep by the time they reached his bedside, and apparently completely unconcerned by the fact that he was in hospital. He seemed far more interested in quizzing his father about a promised outing.

'*Dormire,*' murmured his father patiently as he smoothed a soothing hand over tousled dark hair.

Lissa watched, entranced, as he tried to persuade little Taddeo to go to sleep. He was such a very masculine man and yet he was so gentle with his young son.

The two of them were so similar that she would have known that they were father and son without being told. They both had the same dark brown eyes fringed by impossibly long lashes and the same dark hair prone to unruly curls.

Their skin was the same dark golden colour, and Taddeo would probably one day sport the same dark shadow of an emerging beard that she could see on his father's jaw.

Even the shape of the jaw was similar, lean and slightly angular for all that the child was so much younger, and they both possessed the same knack of smiling with their eyes as well as their mouths.

Her eyes were travelling from one to the other, silently comparing and contrasting while she watched the interaction between father and son. Finally, one set of dark lashes drooped for the last time and a gentle kiss was pressed to a tousled head.

The sight of the man's lean tanned fingers sent a shaft of something close to jealousy through Lissa when she saw how tenderly they cupped the curve of Taddeo's little cheek, and she was startled by the unexpected feeling.

This isn't what you want, she reminded herself sharply as she took a step backwards from the loving scene. Don't let your guard down if you want to protect your heart. Don't get involved, no matter how enticing the temptation.

'Have you lived in Italy very long?' he asked when they were finally on their way.

Lissa gave a silent sigh of relief at the thought that she wasn't going to have to try to start a conversation. At least he was willing to make the effort.

'Actually, it's my first visit,' she admitted. 'I've been wanting to come for years...all my life, in fact.'

'So this is why you have learned to speak Italian?' he demanded, reverting to his own tongue but speaking rather slower than usual to accommodate her. 'In the hope that one day you would be able to visit?'

Lissa laughed and took his lead, switching to her slightly rusty Italian. 'Not quite. I learned to speak Italian so that I could talk to my grandmother. When I was small, I thought Nonna couldn't understand English. It was years before I realised that she didn't miss a thing in either language!'

He laughed with her. 'So this is just a brief holiday, to get a taste of Italy?' he suggested.

She'd given him the name of her hotel before they'd set off, so Lissa could see how he would have come to that conclusion.

'Partly,' she agreed, 'but also to explore this part of the country because it was the area Nonna's family came from.'

'So, you're going to have a very busy week sightseeing. It was lucky for Taddeo that you had a few minutes spare to visit the beach. If you hadn't been there…'

'Then someone else would have taken care of him,' she said, slightly uncomfortable with the open emotion in his voice at the thought of his son's accident. 'You know how much Italian people love children. Those people offered to help me get him off the beach and transport him to hospital without hesitation, lending towels, belts and even that surfboard to protect his back.'

'Even so, I thank you…' He paused with a frown and concentrated for a second on parking his car in front of the hotel then turned to face her. 'How can I thank you properly if I can't even remember the name in your passport?' He held out his hand. 'I am Matteo Aldarini, at your service and for ever in your debt.'

'Melissa Swift,' Lissa supplied, along with her hand, disappointed but not surprised that her name hadn't registered in the heat of the moment.

'Melissa. Sweet as honey,' he murmured as he wrapped long fingers around hers.

Suddenly she was aware that the two of them were alone in the intimacy of the darkened car and all she could think of was the contact between their palms and his dark eyes looking down into hers.

CHAPTER TWO

MATTEO'S hand felt warm and strong, but the strength was carefully tempered…unlike some men Lissa knew who took a delight in grinding her bones together in a show of masculine power.

She'd only met the man a short while ago under the most stressful of conditions but she had a feeling that he would never need to resort to such petty tricks to prove his masculinity.

But it was his eyes that held her captivated, their dark brown depths almost black in the shadowed interior of the car as he gazed at her.

'Today was a dreadful day after a dreadful night,' he murmured, his words taking on a distracted air. 'You might have heard that one of the local hotels has apparently had an outbreak of food poisoning. Some patients were coming to us so sick that they were already dehydrated, but as fast as we found beds for them and put fluids into them, more people arrived.'

He shook his head with a soft groan and dropped it back against the headrest but instead of releasing her hand, he tightened his fingers around hers, almost as if he needed the contact.

'I was still trying to organise the last group and waiting for the victims of a car crash to arrive,' he continued with the suspicion of a smile at the corner of his mouth, 'when a bossy woman in a swimming costume carried my unconscious son into the hospital and started to tell me my job.'

24

'I didn't!' she objected automatically, not sure that she liked the idea that he thought she was bossy.

The fact that he'd noticed what she'd been wearing was a different matter and his mention of it brought a swift wash of heat to her cheeks.

At least he couldn't still see her costume. It was well hidden under the oversized white coat he'd found for her. For all that it was summer in Italy, by this time of night she could have been feeling rather chilly, not to say embarrassed, running around in beachwear.

'Well…thank you for giving me a lift.' She hurried into speech, suddenly realising that he was probably waiting for her to remember her manners. She tried to pull her hand away but he was apparently as reluctant to release her as she was to be released.

'I would like to see you again,' he said in a husky voice, and her heart gave a silly skip. Had he been affected by the same feeling of attraction, unwelcome though it was?

'Of course, it will depend on the situation at the hospital,' he continued apologetically. 'We are really far too small to deal with large outbreaks of anything major. In spite of the holidaymakers, for half of the year this is just a quiet little town, but I would like the chance to thank you for taking care of Taddeo.'

She was still lecturing herself for her presumption as she let herself into her room.

'Of *course* he was only suggesting taking you out as a thank you for helping his son,' she scolded as she stripped off the baggy white coat and made her way to the shower. 'Do you really think a man like that would be hard up for company? He's hardly the type to be interested in short-term relationships with summer visitors—not like those lads on the beach.'

She'd tried to save face by telling him that thanks weren't necessary but he'd been adamant. In the end, they'd left it that he would contact her when his work permitted.

Silently, she had decided that she would be 'too busy' to take him up on the invitation. He was an attractive and clearly very intelligent man and she would probably have thoroughly enjoyed spending an evening with him. Except…her reaction to the idea that he might be interested in her was ringing warning bells inside her head, reminding her that the last thing she wanted while she was in Italy was to get involved in a relationship…even a very short-term one.

She'd intended staying under the shower until she was utterly waterlogged but a few minutes later she was out and towelling her hair dry, too restless to unwind even under the steaming spray.

The evening was still relatively young by Italian standards, but she didn't really know what she wanted to do.

The idea of going out to a restaurant by herself didn't appeal somehow, and neither did dancing at the disco at the hotel at the other end of the parade. She'd stuck her head around the door last night and realised that she would probably be one of the oldest women in the room. Their average age seemed to be little more than eighteen, and as for the music…

Lissa sighed then grimaced, remembering the days when her parents used to complain about her own choice of music. Did this mean that she was rapidly becoming middle-aged at only twenty-eight years of age?

She pulled on some lightweight trousers and a cotton top then reached for the phone, resigned to the idea of room service and a book. It wouldn't do her any harm to have an early night after all the excitement of the day. She could start her holiday afresh tomorrow and hopefully be in a better frame of mind for it.

'Here we are again,' Lissa muttered as she flopped back on her towel, her sunglasses firmly in position.

It was actually two days since Taddeo's accident, but everything around her looked and sounded exactly the same…even the ice-cream van playing 'Greensleeves'.

It wasn't that the accident had put her off the idea of spending time on the beach; she hadn't been particularly keen in the first place. In fact, she'd picked up some of the literature supplied in her room that detailed the various local attractions, and had spent the intervening time exploring a little.

The trouble was, finding the village where her grandmother had grown up wasn't nearly as satisfying without someone to share it with. Nor was her enjoyment of a particularly stunning view or the series of ancient frescos she'd discovered in a tiny church.

If all had gone as she'd expected, there should have been two of them spending their days, and their nights, together.

'Sightseeing on my own was a bit of a washout,' she muttered under her breath as she put the bottle of sunscreen away in her bag. 'Perhaps I'll have a bit more luck getting into the holiday mood with all these happy people all around me.'

She rolled over onto her stomach and propped her chin on her folded arms while she gazed around.

'It's uncanny,' she murmured as her eyes went from one group to another. 'It's almost as if the world has stood still since I was here the first time. Absolutely nothing has changed while I've been away.'

There were the same family groups, the same honeymooners still besotted with each other, the same group of predatory young men eyeing the scantily clad girls giggling their way across the beach.

'No. Something *has* changed!' she exclaimed under her breath in mock surprise when she heard the accents of the target of the young men's comments. 'They're after new prey today—Scandinavian, perhaps?'

She wondered idly what had happened to the group of English girls being pursued last time she was here. Had they succumbed to the false smiles and well-practised lines, or had they seen through them in time?

'*Signorina?*' said a voice nearby. '*Mi scusi. Sei medica?*'

Lissa groaned silently as she rolled over and sat up. That was all she needed…another medical problem on a beach this far from proper hospital facilities. It must be someone who had recognised her from the other day.

She looked up at the young woman standing in front of her and suddenly realised that she recognised her.

'Maddelena!' she exclaimed, rising to her feet and finding herself wrapped in a fervent hug. 'How is Taddeo? Is he well?'

'*Sì.* He is well. We have brought him back to the beach with the whole family so that he will have good memories. Come and see.' She grabbed Lissa's hand and gestured towards the other side of the beach. 'He is over there with my mother. Come. You must join us.'

Lissa paused just long enough to grab her belongings then threaded her way through the various groups of holidaymakers towards an older woman waving a welcoming hand.

Introductions were made and Lissa found herself
once more enveloped in an enthusiastic embrace.

'What would we have done if you hadn't been here
to take care of our Taddeo?' Maddelena's mother exclaimed. 'How can we thank you enough?'

Lissa tried to downplay her contribution, but she
wasn't having it.

'No, no! We think you're a heroine!' she exclaimed,
gesturing towards the rest of the family for confirmation. 'Please…sit. Join us!'

It wasn't long before they were also trying to bully
her into joining them for some fast and furious games
on the beach. Maddelena's brothers and sisters and
cousins were numerous enough to form two complete
opposing teams.

With Taddeo only recently released from hospital, it
was inadvisable for him to be involved in quite that
much rough and tumble, so Lissa opted for keeping
Taddeo occupied with Maddelena's mother.

Soon enough the whole family rejoined them on the
array of blankets and deck-chairs for the most sump-
tuous of picnics and a lazy hour of recuperation while
she was regaled with numerous tales of family misdeeds
and successes.

It was no hardship to listen when she realised just
how often Matteo Aldarini's name was included, in
spite of the fact that he wasn't actually a member of the
family.

'That's my daddy,' Taddeo had announced proudly
the first time it had happened and she'd smiled at him.
She'd been quite surprised to find out that although the
youngster couldn't remember much of the accident, he
seemed to remember her quite clearly from her visit to
his bedside in the paediatric ward.

'He told me you carried me to his hospital on a surf-board when I hit my head,' Taddeo continued, chattering so brightly that it was obvious that he'd suffered few after-effects from his mishap. 'I fell on those rocks.' He pointed at the wicked piles of broken limestone that could so easily have been the cause of his death.

Unfortunately, the sparkle in his eyes suggested that he was the sort of daredevil child whose accident wouldn't put him off the next reckless challenge.

'Who's going swimming?' demanded one of the cousins and there was a noisy response as everyone erupted from their lazy relaxation.

'Will you swim with me?' Taddeo demanded with a grin. 'I'm good. I bet I can race you.'

A quick glance at Maddelena confirmed that he'd been cleared to swim.

'I'll look after him,' Lissa promised and they were off across the beach at a run.

He launched himself into the waves with a shriek almost as soon as the water came up to his knees and it was soon obvious that his words hadn't been an idle boast. He wouldn't have to be able to swim much faster before he *could* beat her, legitimately. She'd only had to shorten her stroke slightly to allow him to pull ahead of her.

'You swim like a fish!' she exclaimed when they came up for air at the float anchored a little way out from shore. 'How old were you when you learned?'

'My daddy took me in the sea when I was just a baby. Only one year old. He said I was like a baby frog.'

'Taddeo the tadpole,' she said in English and chuckled, remembering that 'Taddy' was the nickname her mother had called her when she'd been learning to swim.

'What is a tadpole?' he demanded. She racked her brain for a moment but couldn't remember the Italian word although she was sure her grandmother must have taught her once upon a time.

'I'll tell you when we go back on the beach,' she promised, knowing that there was a dictionary in her bag. 'Are you going to race me back? I need to practise.'

She could see that several of the younger members of the family had started to build an ambitious sand castle and thought that would probably be better for the youngster than too much swimming. At least he would be no more than a few steps from the blankets if he grew tired.

Not that he seemed lacking in energy as he ploughed his way through the water beside her.

Lissa was watching him so closely that she didn't see another figure approaching so that when the water burst into a fountain beside her and Taddeo's body was thrust right up into the air she gave a shriek and sank under the surface.

She'd swallowed several mouthfuls and was coughing and spluttering by the time she surfaced to find Taddeo suspended from his father's hands and screeching with delight.

'I am *so* sorry,' his father said remorsefully as he reached out a hand to support her, Taddeo held against one broad shoulder with the other. 'I wanted to surprise my son and I didn't realise you hadn't seen me coming.'

She couldn't speak for a moment, having to concentrate all her energies on drawing her next breath without coughing.

'Are you all right? Do you want me to help you to the beach?' He must have put the child back in the water because now he had pulled her into his arms and was supporting her against his body.

Lissa shook her head as she heaved in another breath and realised with gratitude that it wasn't going to trigger another bout.

'I'll be all right,' she gasped and looked up into his face for the first time, straight into the dark intensity of deep brown eyes shot with unexpected streaks of gold.

Even in his car she hadn't been this close to him and when she realised just how much contact there was between their nearly naked bodies she grew still.

As she was still out of her depth, he was supporting her in the water and she could feel the movement of every muscle in his powerful legs and lean torso as he controlled their combined weight. And he was so warm, his skin a deep bronze against her lighter gold with a dark swathe of wet hair spread right across the width of his chest.

'I...I'm all right,' she stammered and tried to lean away from the disturbing contact, but there was nothing to push against except him and her legs tangled between his, making the contact even more intimate. 'If you let me go, I'll swim back to shore.'

She glanced in that direction and saw that Taddeo had already reached the beach and joined the sand-castle construction crew.

'But what if I don't want to let you go?' he murmured in a husky voice and tightened his arms fractionally.

Her eyes flew back to his in surprise. *Not* want to let her go? What was he saying?

'Some of my ancestors were fishermen,' he continued, the deep rumble of his voice reaching her through the contact between their bodies as much as through the air. She almost felt as if she was aware of him with

every fibre of her body. 'If a fisherman rescues a mer-
maid he would never just let her go without making
sure she was all right. Then, if he's lucky, she'll reward
him for taking care of her.'

'You want a reward?' she whispered, the words
barely louder than the sound of the water around their
bodies as she tried to come to terms with the idea that
he might be flirting with her.

It took several seconds before she realised that her
own question had sounded flirtatious, and that he'd
taken it that way.

'Of course I want a reward,' he asserted warmly, his
eyes flicking from her eyes to her mouth and back again.

Lissa's tongue moistened lips gone suddenly dry and
she realised that for the first time in several weeks the
idea of kissing a man was appealing…this man.

'Come out with me for a meal,' he demanded suddenly and she blinked.

'A meal?' she repeated unsteadily, aghast at just how
disappointed she was that he hadn't kissed her. 'But…'

'I want to thank you properly for what you did for
my son, so…may I collect you this evening?'

Gratitude.

Her spirits fell and drowned around her. Of course,
the only reason why he was asking her out was out of
gratitude for helping his son. How could she possibly
have thought he was interested in her personally? He
would have done the same if she'd been a man.

'But won't you be on duty?' she asked, grabbing for
the first excuse she could while she turned away from
him and slid out of his arms. It was so easy this time
that she knew he hadn't tried to stop her.

'The hospital has finally given me some time off for
good behaviour,' he said as he swam smoothly and si-

lently beside her, easily keeping pace with her more nervous strokes. 'So…will seven-thirty suit you? Taddeo will be going to bed early as he's still officially recuperating.'

The part of her that had been so recently hurt wanted to turn him down with a pleasant excuse, but the rest of her, the part that had come to vibrant life when he'd wrapped her tightly against his body, was urging her to accept.

What else have you got to look forward to this evening? said an annoying little voice inside her head. Why turn down the invitation to share a meal with a handsome man, especially as you know in advance that he sees it merely as a way of repaying a debt? It isn't as if there's any danger of becoming involved in a relationship with him. You're nothing more than chance acquaintances, after all.

'Make it eight,' she countered as her feet finally touched solid ground and she stood up to wade away from him through the shallows. 'Taddeo told me he's looking forward to his daddy reading a story to him tonight.'

She walked over to retrieve her towel, overwhelmingly conscious of his eyes following her, but her deliberate mention of his son had worked very effectively as a reminder.

For all the forbidden attraction she felt towards him, she was nothing more than a transient holidaymaker and he was the local doctor with a little son to consider. There was no way their two lives could ever do more than touch fleetingly.

'There is a gentleman waiting for you in Reception,' the voice had said over the phone and Lissa's hands were shaking visibly as she smoothed them one last time over the dress she'd chosen.

It wasn't that she was uncertain about the suitability of the style or its fit; the honey-coloured slip of silk was cut on fluid lines and was close to perfect. After all, her whole holiday wardrobe had been chosen with just such events in mind.

They just hadn't been chosen for her to go out with *this* man.

It didn't seem to matter that she kept reminding herself that she'd decided to steer clear of men for the foreseeable future, or that the offer of a meal was by way of showing his gratitude. For the last couple of hours her pulse and respiration had rocketed each time she'd thought about his invitation, and much though she felt she ought to cancel, she knew she had no intention of doing so.

'He's waiting,' she muttered, conscious of time passing while she dithered, and a lifetime of punctuality wouldn't allow her to delay any more.

'You already know he's totally out of bounds, so there's absolutely no danger in spending an evening with him,' she reminded herself, resorting to a pep talk in the descending lift. 'He's just a man.'

The doors slid open and her first sight of him gave the lie to her assertion. Her knees grew weak just at the sight of him waiting for her in the reception area and she had to admit that Matteo Aldarini wasn't *just* anything.

It really wasn't fair, she wailed silently as she gazed at him in something close to despair.

He was wearing dark formal trousers that accentuated the long lean length of his legs and his slim hips, and an open-necked white shirt that contrasted starkly with the bronze of his skin. The suit jacket was casually suspended over one shoulder by the loop, but there was nothing casual in the expression in his eyes as they travelled over her from head to toe and back again.

'*Che bella!*' he murmured finally as he took her hand and lifted it to his lips, then brought it through the crook of his arm. He turned to usher her towards the door without taking his eyes from her. 'I will be the envy of every man tonight.'

There was a heat in his gaze that almost seemed to scorch where it touched and she was quite grateful for the shadows once they were outside. Perhaps he wouldn't see the heat in her cheeks that betrayed just how much he was affecting her.

The meal was everything she could have wished, and more.

How could she fail to enjoy an evening spent in the company of such an attentive host? From the moment they were shown to their secluded table and he held her chair for her everything was so perfect it was almost a fantasy.

It didn't matter that she'd sworn never to be swayed by externals again. She'd already had her trust broken that way once.

But somehow this was different. The surroundings, the food, the music…everything was wonderful, but it all paled into insignificance before the man beside her.

His conversation was witty and erudite and not only did he take the time to ask her questions about herself, he actually listened to her answers with obvious interest.

It had been so long since that had happened that she

felt herself relaxing and opening up like some rare flower under the warmth of his regard.

All too soon their meal was over and he was ushering her out into the starry darkness.

He could have wrapped an arm around her shoulders, making the excuse that the evening air might seem chill after the warmth of the restaurant. To her disappointment he seemed perfectly content to walk beside her, their only contact her hand on his arm.

He paused as they neared her hotel, just a few minutes farther along the sea front.

'Is it too late for you to take a walk with me?' he asked quietly with a gesture towards the beach beside them, and she had to suppress the urge to shout her agreement. She certainly wasn't ready for their evening to end just yet.

He must have taken her hesitation for uncertainty.

'Of course, if you'd rather I took you straight back to your hotel...'

'No!' she exclaimed, then added hastily, 'No, a walk would be nice after all that food. I wouldn't be able to sleep yet.'

He turned towards the nearest path that led in a shallow zigzag down to the sand.

It was hard to believe that it was the same busy, noisy place that she'd visited earlier that day.

By night it was all but silent and deserted, only nature providing the sounds.

At the end of the zigzag he stopped to slip off his shoes and socks and roll up his trouser legs.

'Shall I help you?' He crouched in front of her and wrapped warm fingers around one ankle.

She braced a hand on his shoulder and slipped each sandal off in turn, glad that she'd decided to go barelegged tonight. It wouldn't have fitted into the moonlit fantasy to have to struggle to remove tights or stockings in front of him.

'We can leave our shoes here,' he suggested, placing both pairs in a patch of dark shadow beside some rocks and folding his jacket on top of them before he straightened up again and held out a silent hand.

In unspoken agreement they turned towards the water and walked until their feet found the hard-packed sand before they changed direction to follow the edge of the waves.

The sea was calm tonight, far calmer than her turbulent thoughts. Inside her head an argument was raging, with one part of her longing to spend more time with this fascinating charismatic man, while the other urged her to keep her vow of caution and restraint.

There was no argument about the fact that she was regretting that their evening together was nearly over.

They'd walked all the way to the rocks at the far end of the beach before he paused beside her to stare out over the sea. Without a word being spoken they stood side by side, the breeze gently fluttering hair and clothing, and she was aware of a strange feeling of contentment.

'I wasn't ready for the evening to end,' he said quietly, finally breaking the silence. 'I hope you don't mind.'

Lissa was so startled to hear him voice her own feelings that she wasn't quick enough to keep a check on her tongue.

'Neither was I,' she admitted fervently, then could have kicked herself. What on earth was wrong with her? Over the last few weeks she thought she'd become adept at hiding her thoughts and feelings from others.

Surely an evening in his company wasn't enough for her to lose that hard-won control. She'd really hoped that she'd learned not to reveal her thoughts so impetuously.

How humiliating to lapse *now*, she groaned silently, turning her face away. And he was probably only being his usual polite self, telling her what he thought she wanted to hear...

'Ah, Melissa, it's more than that!' he exclaimed, breaking into her scrambled thoughts as he turned her back to face him. 'Tell me that you feel it, too—this crazy attraction between us.'

He captured each of her hands in his and pressed them against the soft cotton covering his chest.

She was so overwhelmed by his unexpected exclamation and so aware of the warmth of his body and the rhythmic beat of his heart that she almost missed his next words.

'Do you not know that ever since I saw you standing there in the hospital, all long bare legs and big dark eyes, you have filled my mind...my thoughts.' He brought her hands up to his lips and pressed a kiss to each.

Lissa was lost for words, her own heart beating so loudly that she was sure he must be able to hear it over the sound of the sea.

'But this is so crazy,' he continued, his tone almost one of exasperation. 'We're not teenagers to be overtaken by lust in the blink of an eye. We're both responsible professional people. This can't be real.'

'You're right. It *is* crazy,' she said, trying to hang on to logic in the face of almost overwhelming temptation. How was she supposed to resist when he was looking at her like that?

'Matt, we only met a few days ago and under the most fraught conditions.' She tried to pull her hands free but he wouldn't release her, forcing her to stay close enough to breathe in the musky warmth of his body. It certainly didn't help as she tried to put her thoughts into words.

'I'm just a visitor here,' she continued, trying to be logical. 'And I certainly didn't come here looking for a holiday fling.' Ah, but the thought of it was so beguiling. For the first time, she could almost identify with those groups of girls she'd been watching.

'I never thought it for a moment,' he agreed gently. 'I've seen the young men lurking on the beach and in the square. It's probably the same in the discos and nightclubs, although it's years since I last bothered to go.'

It was almost uncanny how closely his thoughts had mirrored her own and when the silence grew between them she somehow knew that he was wondering where they went from here, too. He was still holding her hands against his chest and she drew comfort from the fact that he hadn't released her.

'Can we be friends?' she suggested quietly, but without much hope that he would agree. He was such a strong, decisive sort of man, so vibrant, that she was afraid he wouldn't be interested in half-measures like friendship.

CHAPTER THREE

'I DON'T think mere friendship will be possible between a man and a woman,' Matt had said in a husky voice that had thrilled and dismayed Lissa all at once. 'Especially when there is so much attraction between them.'

His softly accented voice had had an effect all its own as they'd stood in the moonlit darkness of the Italian night. She'd seen from his shadowy expression that he hadn't been happy with his thoughts and had found herself holding her breath as she'd waited for him to finish. She could hardly have blamed him if he'd wanted nothing more to do with her, but something deep inside her had wanted to know more about the effect he had on her.

Not just the physical awareness, that had been easy to understand. It had been the indefinable 'something' she'd felt when he'd been near her...

'But if that is what you wish,' he'd conceded softly, 'then that is how it must be.'

His words had repeated themselves so often in her head that they had become part of her dreams and her nightmares.

At the time, she'd been so relieved that he hadn't dismissed the idea out of hand that she hadn't commented or asked any questions. It hadn't occurred to her until much later that she'd tacitly agreed to being attracted to him.

Had he been one of the unscrupulous Lotharios she'd

41

seen on the beach, he would probably have taken advantage of that attraction in spite of her misgivings.

The fact that he hadn't even tried was either proof of the fact that he was honourable enough to stick to their agreement, or that she'd effectively killed his interest.

It didn't stop him being a pleasant, albeit platonic companion but it left her with a growing dilemma. The more time she spent with him, the more she enjoyed it, but the more she found herself reacting to his slightest touch. Unfortunately, he didn't seem to feel the same way.

Now, nearly a week later, she was more than tempted to push the boundaries of their 'arrangement' but had no idea how to do it, or even if Matt still wanted anything more than her company.

Not that he'd given her any hint that he was bored; he was far too much of a gentleman for that.

She certainly wasn't complaining about the turn her holiday had taken. There had been no time to lie on the beach wondering how to fill the hours when she knew Taddeo was going to arrive at any minute demanding her attention.

Each day they would explore the rock pools left behind by the tide, then embark on the building of yet another of her young friend's individually designed sand castles.

Her swimming 'lesson' came next, as he coached her about her style so that, 'if you practise hard enough, one day you might be able to swim as fast as me'.

Lissa hated to admit it, but her swimming had actually improved since she'd started taking his advice. Tonight, she would have to remember to thank Matt for the secondhand tuition.

Just the thought of seeing Matt was enough to send

her pulse rate up several notches and put a smile on her face.

Spending so much time in his company was rapidly becoming one of the most frustrating things she'd ever done, but she'd never enjoyed herself so much.

After the chaos of the food-poisoning episode, his workload had apparently settled down into the usual madness of the summer season, but at least he'd been able to take his proper off-duty hours for the last few days. And it seemed as if he was just as keen to spend those hours with her as she was to have his company.

Several afternoons they'd taken Taddeo with them when they'd gone exploring the countryside, looking for the places she remembered her grandmother talking about.

Some areas were still so relatively unspoiled that she felt she could almost be seeing them exactly as Nonna had when she'd been a girl.

Away from the coast, the region was largely a gently rolling plateau covered by farmland and pasture. The wheat fields had already been harvested, this late in the season, but some of the olive groves were still a hive of activity.

Taddeo was more interested in the land closer to the coast with its belt of orchards. It was almost impossible to drive past a wayside stall without giving in to his pleas to stop to sample some of the luscious peaches, apples or plums.

But it was the evenings she enjoyed the most, when she could have Matt all to herself.

Already he'd taken her to an open-air concert and an art gallery as well as a selection of the finest restaurants the area had to offer. Finally, she'd had to put her foot down.

'I can understand that your Italian pride won't let me pay for you,' she'd said last night when they'd arrived at yet another obviously expensive bistro. 'But I can't let you pay for me all the time either.'

'You don't enjoy being taken out for a meal?' He had seemed almost affronted and she'd hastened to smooth his ruffled feathers.

'I love being taken out for a meal, especially when the company is good. But I don't need expensive entertainment and wining and dining all the time. I also like spending time peacefully...away from other people,' she'd explained, hoping she hadn't sounded ungrateful. 'I have enjoyed every minute of the last week, but sometimes it's good to relax informally rather than having to dress up to go out.'

So here she was, dressed to order in a pair of lightweight trousers and a shirt and waiting for her escort to arrive to take her to a mystery destination. She had a fleece jacket in her bag and a pair of trainers in case her sandals were too flimsy.

She was filled with a mixture of guilt and excitement at the promise this evening held. Excitement that they were going to be spending time together and guilt that she'd almost engineered the fact that they would be alone.

A gentle tattoo at her door made her heart leap into her mouth and she hurried across to open it.

Matt bit his tongue and concentrated on drawing in a steadying breath.

What was she trying to do to him with her dark hair tumbling around her shoulders? Her body looked slender and willowy in those dark trousers and as for what that white silk shirt did to her skin...

It had been a week since he'd agreed to limit the two of them to friendship and he'd regretted it the very second he'd opened his mouth to say the words.

How was he supposed to stay sane when every hormone in his body ached at the thought of her, and as for spending time in her company...

It was obvious that the five years since he'd wanted to be close to a woman had been far too long. It was true that the events surrounding Taddeo's birth had left him more than wary, and the excuse that he had a son to care for was legitimate up to a point, but the way he felt at Lissa's slightest touch was turning him inside out.

Was it just that she was forbidden fruit? He knew that she would only be in San Vittorio for a little while longer, and that she wasn't the type to indulge in a mindless holiday romance, but...if he'd taken her to bed would the urgency have faded...disappeared?

He looked into those dark honey eyes and when he felt the familiar tension begin to rise he knew the very idea was crazy. Making love with her once would only make him want to do it again, and it didn't help that he could see two beds at the other side of the room. If he didn't say something *now*, he could end up ruining the little they had together.

'Ready?' One dark eyebrow echoed the husky-voiced question and Lissa had to suppress the urge to groan aloud.

There he was, dressed in a pair of jeans that were just old enough to outline his lower body like a second skin and with a T-shirt that showed off an upper body fit for the cover of a bodice-ripper, and he asked her if she was ready? She wondered if he realised just how ready she was to forget all about her stupid idea of restricting their relationship to being friends.

What she really wanted to do was drag him into the room and finally get her hands on the body she'd been ogling for days. Even in her dreams she'd been running her hands over those sun-bronzed muscles and she was longing to find out if the body under those clothes could possibly feel as perfect as her imagination had been telling her.

And she didn't want to stop with touching. When she had him naked, she wanted the chance to find out just how many of her increasingly heated fantasies they could fulfil before they were both too exhausted to move.

'Lissa? Are you ready?' he prompted with the beginning of a frown and she hastily dragged her thoughts back from forbidden territory.

'Um…yes,' she croaked, regretfully calling her imagination to heel for the evening. 'Are you going to tell me where we're going?'

He shook his head, his smile just as wicked as his son's when he was up to mischief.

'You'll have to wait and see. Don't be so impatient.'

'What about giving me some clues?' she begged as they entered the lift, almost as if she were Taddeo trying to work his way round his father. 'Is it somewhere we've been before? I'm not dressed for going somewhere smart.'

'I've brought us a picnic, so you're dressed perfectly. Now, no more clues, other than it's not anywhere that you've been before and it's somewhere I haven't been for a long time.'

He had his car waiting outside the front of the hotel and in no time they were on their way.

Lissa could tell when the road began to twist and climb through a band of thick forest that they were heading inland, and that they were using one of the older roads in this part of the country. It almost looked more like the Black Forest region of Germany than the traditional image of the parched southern half of Italy.

They had been travelling for nearly an hour when Matt indicated and turned off onto a rough track. The going was much slower here as he took care not to damage the car on the loose rocks littering the track. Slowly the road rose out of the pine trees so that the headlights began to pick up the more rugged outline of rocky outcrops between cultivated fields and orchards.

The way he was peering out through the windscreen gave the impression that he wasn't completely certain where he was going and Lissa had a momentary bout of uncertainty. This was obviously a very remote, rugged area. What if he was lost? a little voice whispered. What if the car broke down? The road was too rural to see much traffic.

She dismissed her qualms. He had said that he had been here before and she trusted him to take care of her.

Finally, apparently in the middle of nowhere, he drew to a halt and switched off the engine and the lights.

'We're here,' he announced into a darkness that was more intense than anything she'd ever known before.

'Where, exactly?' she prompted nervously as he opened his door, hoping he wasn't going to disappear from sight. She certainly wouldn't be able to find him if he did.

'Wait and see,' he said again with an unexpected chuckle as he opened her door and took her elbow.

'Wait and *see*?' she repeated in disbelief as she found

his hand and held on tightly, ignoring the familiar frisson of awareness at his touch. 'I can't see a thing.'

'Close your eyes and count to ten,' he advised, threading the fingers of one hand between hers, the other occupied with the basket he'd taken off the back seat. 'Your eyes are accustomed to using the car headlights to see. Give them time to adjust to the lower light levels.'

'*Lower* light levels? *No* light levels is more accurate,' she muttered under her breath while she stood obediently with her eyes shut.

With one hand clasped firmly in his she discovered that she wasn't in the least afraid. It was the first time she'd deliberately prolonged their touch since her capricious edict that they should restrict themselves to friendship, and she was far too aware of the contact between them to waste her energy on being afraid of the dark. 'Friends,' she reminded herself in a stern mutter. 'It's just a friendship,'

'Hey! Have you counted to ten or are you too busy mumbling?' he demanded impatiently, a smile in his voice. He'd been strangely subdued towards the end of their journey, but now he seemed almost eager to reach their destination.

'I'm counting. I'm counting. Eight, nine, ten.'

She opened her eyes and gazed around briefly, but although she could now distinguish the shadowy outlines of their surroundings far more clearly, there was absolutely nothing to see. No house. No road. In fact, absolutely nothing that looked manmade. Then she stared upwards.

'Wow!' she breathed in awe. 'I've never seen so many stars. There are millions of them, and they're so big and bright that they almost seem close enough to touch.'

'This is what the sky used to look like when I was a boy,' he said softly, his hushed voice fitting the wild majesty of their surroundings. 'That was before all the improvements that brought so much artificial light into the night. In the cities, sometimes there are so many streetlights that you can hardly see the stars at all.'

'How did you know about this place?' She was still looking up and starting to pick out some of the constellations she'd learned about at school.

'We used to live not far from here. Just over that rise.' He pointed and she found that she could quite easily pick out the outline of the rocky terrain nearby. The low level of natural light was certainly enough to pick her way in his wake as he led her up the sharp rise.

'Here. Sit.' He patted a weatherworn rock. 'Catch your breath.'

He, of course, was hardly breathing heavily, let alone panting after that short scramble up the track, but he still sat himself down beside her.

'Listen,' he whispered, and she had to concentrate to ignore the fact that he'd just captured her hand again.

'It sounds as if we're still at the coast,' she exclaimed in surprise. She'd been so certain that they'd been travelling inland. 'I can still hear the sea.'

He chuckled, the husky sound wrapping warmly around her in the darkness.

'That's not the sea. That's the wind in the pine trees.' He leant closer, putting his arm around her shoulder as he pointed down in the direction they'd come. 'Do you see the cluster of lights over there?'

Lissa was very conscious of the contact between

them as she peered into the distance and had to concentrate before she saw a vague orange glow. 'I see it.'

'That's San Vittorio, and over there…' he turned and pointed behind them '…if the weather's clear, we're high enough, here, so you can just see the lights of Altavetta between the hills.'

The two towns seemed very far away.

'It's almost as if we're sitting on top of the world,' she murmured, missing the warm weight around her shoulders now he'd taken his arm away to open the basket on the smaller rock in front of them. 'All I can hear is the sound of the wind in the trees and the cicadas. Do your parents still live up here? I can't hear the sound of any animals.'

'They died some time ago,' Matt admitted softly, looking up at her from the candle he was lighting in a dark blue glass container. 'They had come to my *consegna delle lauree*…when I became a doctor.' He paused, apparently lost for the word.

'Graduation?' she suggested.

'Exactly so. Graduation.' He paused as though fixing the word in his memory, or was he regretting starting the topic? Lissa didn't know whether to interrupt. The last thing she'd intended was that he should resurrect unhappy memories, but he continued before she could decide.

'They were on their way back here after the celebrations when their car went off the road,' he said in a rough voice that showed his feelings far more than his economical words. 'No one saw it so I never knew what happened. I could only be relieved that they died together and that they died quickly.'

'Oh, Matteo. I'm so sorry.'

Somehow, it seemed right to call him by his full

name at a moment of revelation such as that. She'd
turned to face him—was almost touching him on their
rocky perch—but he was looking out towards the en-
circling darkness. All she could see was a silhouette of
lean planes and hollows but her imagination could easily fill in the details. She'd certainly spent enough time
watching him while he played with his son to be able
to call it to mind.

'What about the rest of your family?' Her voice drew
him back from where his memories had taken him and
he turned to face her again. 'Where do they live?'

'Nowhere,' he said simply and leant forward to retrieve a plate piled high with a selection of cold meats,
all prepared especially to be eaten with the fingers. 'I'm
afraid I'm a rare phenomenon for an Italian. No large
family…just Taddeo and me.'

'But Maddelena… All the cousins…?' He'd told her
that the beautiful young woman wasn't his wife but they
were such a closely knit group that she'd been sure…

'They are the family of a colleague,' he completed,
and she could hear the smile in his voice. 'They just
happen to have hearts big enough to include any number of extra members, no matter that they aren't related.'

'They've certainly made *me* feel welcome, and I'm
only a holiday visitor,' she pointed out.

'You're much more than a holiday visitor, Lissa. You
became much more when you took care of Taddeo.' His
voice was rough and full of feeling and for a moment
she thought he was going to say more, but there was a
rustling sound somewhere close by and his attention
was drawn away sharply.

'What is it?' she whispered when she realised that he

was staring intently at a group of stunted pines only just visible in the darkness.

'I can remember, when I was about five, my grandfather bringing me up here to watch for a wolf,' he said softly, his eyes never wavering. 'They were very rare in this region, even then. I doubt there are any left now, even in such an undisturbed area…'

'A wolf!' Lissa gasped when she could catch her breath. The thought of coming face to face with one of the villains of childhood fairy-tales was so scary that she didn't know whether she should be prepared to run and if so in what direction. 'You think there might be a wolf over there?'

'I doubt if we'd be that lucky, around here.' To her disbelief he sounded almost sad.

'Lucky? To see a wolf?' she squeaked.

He smiled reassuringly. 'Wolves have been the victims of centuries of unwarranted bad press. They live in family groups and generally avoid people but their numbers have dropped because modern farming has robbed them of their natural prey.'

He paused to listen again then shook his head. 'There are some small packs in the national park in the Abruzzi Mountains, but they've become a tourist attraction.' His voice softened. 'I've never forgotten the sight of that male, even though I was only five. He was about the size of a large dog and he was magnificent. All different colours of grey merging from black on his back to nearly silver on his throat and chest so that he seemed almost like a moving shadow…but with such a presence… He really thought he was master of the world.'

'Weren't you frightened?' she demanded. In spite of his attempts at reassurance, her own fear was evident in the rapid pounding of her pulse, her eyes darting around, looking for the slightest sign of movement. 'Why on earth did your grandfather put you in such danger?'

'I was in no danger, especially with my Nonno beside me,' Matt said gently. 'He had been watching the wolves for years and they had grown accustomed to him…especially when he would put meat out for them in hard years when their young might have died. Even so, he'd gradually seen their numbers decrease and he wanted me to see them before they were all gone.'

'What happened?' She was fascinated in spite of herself.

'Nonno whistled, low and gentle, and the wolf stopped and turned his head to look right at us. His eyes were a strange greeny-gold and almost luminous and it was…it was almost as if he was memorising me so that he would know me again. I knew that he meant me no harm and he obviously knew that I was no danger to him because when he walked away he'd changed direction to walk right past us so I could see his mate following him like a paler silver shadow.'

Lissa had been so enthralled by his narrative that she'd completely forgotten her initial fear.

'Did you ever see them again?' She resumed eating, loving the sound of his deep voice in the still of the night and deliberately encouraging him to talk.

'Once, I thought I did, from a distance, when I came back for the funeral of my parents. But I couldn't be sure. There were some feral dogs about, too. Abandoned in the country to fend for themselves by people who'd had to move into the town to find work.'

The conversation moved on and circled through a variety of subjects so that time seemed suspended, almost as if this evening would go on for ever.

In her heart of hearts, Lissa would have to admit that she didn't want this time to end. She could never admit it to a soul, but she was in dire danger of losing her heart to this man, and it seemed as if there was nothing she could do about it.

She dragged her eyes away from him and drew in a steadying breath, hoping to find a measure of common sense at the same time.

The air was cooler this high inland than in the sweltering heat that sometimes blanketed the coast, and as the land began to shed the day's warmth a fitful breeze began to eddy around them. The trees closest to them almost seemed to be whispering secrets to each other. Could they read her mind? Did they know that she would never forget this quiet magical night?

Lissa shivered.

'Ah, Lissa, I'm so sorry. You are getting cold while I ramble on about nothing in particular.' He went to take off his jumper to give to her but she put her hand over his to stay his actions.

'I'm not cold—don't forget, I come from England. We're a hardy race. And anyway, I'm glad you brought me here,' she added and knew it was true. She had learned so much more about the man in this evening together than she ever would have in the midst of the noisy gatherings on the beach.

'I'm glad, too.' He captured her hand and lifted it to his lips to press a kiss to her knuckles. 'It is the first time I've been back here since my parents' funeral. Somehow, I couldn't bear the thought of coming before.'

He didn't say any more, but just those few words were enough to make her feel special; that he should have decided to bring her with him when he made this pilgrimage to his childhood haunt. He made it sound almost as if her presence had been an important part of it.

There had been no repeat of the mysterious sound in the trees by the time they climbed back down to his car with the empty picnic basket and began the journey back towards San Vittorio. Lissa was strangely sad that she would never have a chance to find out if there were still wolves near Matt's childhood home.

They hardly spoke while he drove through the darkness, but the silence between them was so comfortable that there seemed little need for conversation.

The bright lights across the front of the hotel signalled the end of the journey and Lissa was all too conscious of her spirits drooping at the thought that it was also the end of their time together.

Matt drew up outside the front of the hotel and she was just releasing the catch on her seat belt when there was the sound of a high-pitched bleep.

Matt reached for the pager that seemed to accompany him wherever he went and cursed softly under his breath when he read the illuminated display.

'That's a familiar noise,' Lissa commented wryly as he reached for his mobile phone. She fell silent when the call was answered, concentrating on translating his quick-fire Italian.

Her fluency had been growing with each day that she was using the language and it didn't take much for her to understand that there had been some sort of accident involving multiple victims.

'I must get to the hospital,' he announced as soon as he broke the connection. 'A holiday coach has crashed and there could be dozens of people injured. I'm so sorry that our evening must end like this, but there isn't time for me to escort you to your room…'

'Don't be silly,' she said briskly, slotting her belt back into place. 'If you're expecting dozens of people to arrive any minute, then you'd better start driving.'

'But, Lissa—'

Impatiently, she interrupted.

'Come on, Matt! I remember what the hospital was like when you were inundated with those people with food poisoning. A coach crash could be very much worse. You're going to need every pair of hands you can get, and mine are fully trained.'

'You mean, you want to treat the injured?' He seemed quite startled. 'But you're here on holiday and—'

'Give me a break!' she exclaimed. 'Do you think I could sit quietly in my hotel room knowing I could be doing something to help? Please, get driving! There are injured people on their way.'

The urgent tone of her voice seemed to snap him out of his amazement and his brain came to life with a jolt.

'But you aren't employed by the hospital,' he objected, his mind working logically on the unexpected situation even as he gunned the engine and swung out onto the road. 'You can't just expect to walk into the hospital and start treating patients. It would be a recipe for disaster if people only had to *claim* to be qualified to be let loose among the injured.'

'It didn't seem to worry you when I was taking care of the tadpole,' she reminded him, paradoxically pleased that he was not the sort of man who would put present need above patient safety. There was no chance that an unqualified doctor would trick his way into *his* department. 'Anyway, I've already shown you evidence of my British accreditation—'

'Yes, I know, but there are official channels to go through, and—'

'Matt, surely it would be no different if we'd come upon the crash at the side of the road just outside San Vittorio,' she reasoned. 'You certainly wouldn't have expected me to sit in the car and let you get on with it while you did your doctor bit!'

There wasn't time for him to respond as they'd reached the main hospital entrance. They could already see the flashing lights of the first ambulance approaching from the other direction.

He spun the steering-wheel to slot the car swiftly into his assigned space near the emergency department and switched off the engine, one hand already reaching for the door-handle.

'Look, Lissa, I have no authority to give you permission to treat any patient. What happens if something goes wrong? What happens if someone sues you? There must be a thousand forms and protocols to fulfil before—' He broke off at the sound of another approaching ambulance and glanced across with a harried expression as it sped into view.

'Matt, you need my help, even if it comes attached to a pair of English hands instead of Italian ones,' she declared hotly and took off towards the emergency entrance, leaving her words floating back over her shoulder. 'I promise you, I'm properly qualified, and I'll fill in all those wretched forms as soon as there's time, but for now, please, can we get to work?'

Out of the corner of her eye she saw him fling both hands up in the air with an exasperated sound and take off in pursuit.

'If you're not sure of anything, for heaven's sake, give me a shout,' he warned as they ran towards the emergency entrance.

Lissa blinked as they entered a scene that could have been subtitled 'A vision of hell'.

If she'd thought the human misery of dozens of victims of food poisoning had been bad, this was infinitely worse.

There was blood everywhere she looked.

'Here.' Matt thrust a handful of protective clothing at her. 'Plastic aprons and gloves are there.' He pointed as he stripped his own jumper over his head and thrust his arms into a scrub top.

There wasn't time to appreciate the brief glimpse of perfectly bronzed chest. There was too much work to do.

It only took an instant for her to find a corner behind a curtain to do a similar strip-tease—this wasn't the moment to worry about modesty—and then she dived into the fray.

'Who's doing triage, Matt?' she demanded over the cacophony of misery when she rejoined him. He seemed almost like a traffic policeman for a moment, a few swift signals and words directing his human traffic in the most appropriate directions. 'Where do you need me most?'

Almost as she spoke there was a shout from one of the cubicles.

'In there,' he pointed. '*Arresto cardiaco.*'

She didn't need him to translate to know that the patient she was hurrying towards was in imminent heart failure.

The elderly man who met her gaze was struggling to breathe while the young nurse and an even younger medic looked on in horror, apparently too frozen to react.

Years of training took over. It didn't matter that her patient was in no fit state to answer questions—her own expertise should be enough to make a diagnosis in such an extreme situation.

His breathing was worsening by the second, his face turning blue as his body struggled to take in enough oxygen. The veins in his neck were bulging and his trachea had deviated from the midline.

As soon as his shirt was stripped away she could see the start of a livid bruise across one side of his ribs and it came as no surprise when Lissa listened to his chest and found one side ominously silent.

'He has one lung collapsed,' she said, and because she wasn't certain she'd used the correct terminology in Italian she mimed a puncture wound from a broken rib.

'Ah, *si*!' exclaimed the young man who looked hardly old enough to have left school, let alone be in charge of life-and-death situations in a hospital emergency department.

The nurse had obviously understood, too, because she immediately reached for a tray on the well-stocked shelf behind her and ripped off the sealing tapes.

As she reached for the antibacterial soaked wipe to prepare the site, Lissa was very aware that with each breath more air was leaking out from the punctured lung and into the chest cavity. She was going to have to position a needle between the ribs to enable the trapped air to escape and if she didn't get it right first time, there soon wouldn't be any room for the lungs to inflate at all.

She'd done this very thing several times before in

very similar circumstances, but still ran through the process in her head to make sure of the details while the nurse tore open the sterile packaging around the large-bore catheter.

'Second intercostal space, midclavicular line,' she murmured just under her breath as she checked the position. 'Insert the needle along the *upper* border of the rib so you don't puncture the intercostal nerve and artery that run along the lower border. You should be able to feel the needle ''pop'' into the pleural space...'

She looked up and grinned when there was an audible hiss as the air began to escape.

Before she could say anything, the young man leapt into action, connecting the tubing to lead from the needle into a container of water to prevent any air re-entering the chest through the drain.

The nurse handed Lissa several cut lengths of tape and she quickly secured the catheter in position before reaching for the stethoscope again.

'Any problems?' asked a familiar voice and she turned to meet a pair of concerned dark eyes.

'Not so far,' she said with a smile and gestured towards their patient. 'Tension pneumothorax caused by a broken rib puncturing a lung. I think we've got him stable, for the time being.'

'Well done,' Matt said quietly, the tension easing slightly from around his eyes. 'Carlo here has only been with us for about ten days and I don't think he's even seen one before at such close quarters. I hope you gave him a good demonstration. Luckily, most medical terminology has Latin origins, so the vocabulary won't have been too different.'

'*Perfetto!*' exclaimed the young man, warm admiration in his eyes. 'Just like in the book. She even told me exactly what she was doing while she was doing it.'

Lissa felt a wash of heat rise over her face when she realised that her silent recap about the process hadn't been as silent as she'd thought.

'*Mi scusi?*' said a hoarse voice and Lissa felt a hand tugging at her arm. '*Parla inglese?* Does anyone speak English?' her patient asked in a broad Yorkshire accent.

'Yes. I *am* English,' she replied with a smile, quickly bending forwards to stop his struggle to sit up. She checked that the cannula was still safely taped in position. 'Please, lie still. How are you feeling?'

'Bloody awful,' he said bluntly but waved a dismissive hand, clearly concerned about something else entirely. 'Please, have you seen Muriel? My wife. Is she all right?'

'I'll get someone to check,' Lissa promised. 'What's her full name?'

While she was taking the details Matt touched her shoulder.

'I will fetch someone to translate. We are needed more urgently for other people,' he reminded her softly, and left the cubicle.

CHAPTER FOUR

LISSA was greatly in demand over the next couple of hours. Not only did she find out that she was one of the more experienced A and E doctors, she was also able to communicate easily with their patients.

'We were on a coach holiday—the first foreign trip of my life,' explained a bird-like retired headmistress wryly. The analgesia had taken the edge off the pain of two broken legs but hadn't dimmed the edge of her conversational skills. 'Two coaches full of old wrinklies off to see the glories of Italy, and one coach ploughed into the back of the other and tipped them both off the road.'

That explained the who and the how, Lissa thought as she carefully checked the doses she'd administered and initialled her notes. Up till now she'd been far too busy trying to stabilise severely traumatised patients to find out why her countrymen had been involved in such a disaster. There were seven dead already, and at least one gentleman's life was hanging in the balance as a result of a massive heart attack.

Apart from that, there were numerous broken bones and even more stitches still required for nasty gashes. How much worse it would have been if the coach windows hadn't been fitted with the new toughened safety glass. The emergency services would probably still be trying to retrieve bodies from right down the hillside.

'Have you had enough or are you game to do some *cucitura*?' Matt asked when he caught up with her on her way to the central station yet again. He mimed stitching.

'Embroidery?' Lissa suggested with a cheeky grin, deliberately misunderstanding. 'Tapestry?'

'There is enough waiting to make a tapestry,' he agreed grimly. 'And some of the skin is so old and fragile that it is going to be a very long job. You've already been working for hours. Are you sure you wouldn't rather go back to your hotel? It's going to be a very long night.'

Lissa had a sudden memory of the time one of the cats had scratched her grandmother's hand and had torn the skin open almost from her wrist to her knuckles. It had been over a week of care and vigilance before she'd been certain Nonna was healing safely.

'I wouldn't sleep, knowing I'd left the rest of you still working,' she said quietly. She felt a new surge of stamina when she looked up and saw the concern in his eyes and knew it was for her. 'Where do you want me to start?'

It was hours more before the last of the victims had been attended to, and her shoulders were burning from being held in the same position for so long.

She stretched, pulling her elbows towards each other behind her back then stretching both hands towards the ceiling. At least there was the satisfaction of knowing that she'd done her best.

Some wounds had needed dozens of tiny careful stitches to hold the jagged edges neatly together, while others, especially on the thinnest, most delicate skin, had responded best to numerous strips of very narrow adhesive tape.

'Good job I'm on holiday,' quipped one of the ladies when Lissa finished with the last butterfly on a four-inch gash that ran from her wrist up over her forearm. 'At least there's no chance that I'll forget about getting it wet and start on the washing-up.'

'Shame about the swimming, though,' Lissa commiserated and her patient laughed in obvious disbelief.

'At my age?' she scoffed. 'You must be joking—with all those gorgeous young things parading about all but naked! My swimming days are long over, dear.'

'I wouldn't be too sure,' Lissa countered. 'This end of Italy is far less commercialised than the north and doesn't cater nearly so much for the younger end of the market. You wait till you see the age range on the beaches around here before you make a final decision. There's everyone from great-grandmothers to babies in carry-cots. You probably wouldn't even merit a second glance, unless your bathing suit's particularly loud.'

Her patient chuckled. 'The only one I've got is plain navy, not much different from the ones we wore half a century ago,' she admitted with a wry grimace.

'There are plenty of pretty ones in the shops, if you feel like cheering yourself up,' Lissa suggested. 'There are a couple of really good-quality boutiques near the centre of town. You could browse around with some of your friends while you get your courage up to take the beaches by storm.' She carefully hid a smile when she saw the thoughtful expression on the older face.

'Taking a trip round the shops would certainly help to pass the time. And if we did see some costumes we liked… Perhaps a group of us could all go to the beach together…for mutual support,' she mused aloud, then laughed with genuine amusement. 'Can you imagine what the shopkeeper would think if he had a crowd of us coming in all looking like we'd been in some sort of massacre? They'd probably call the police out to ban us from the beach in case we staged a riot!'

'They'd be more likely to get a round of applause for their courage,' Matt suggested later, when Lissa reported the conversation to him. 'All the emergency personnel are amazed by how calm everyone has been, even the seriously injured. They all seem to have been far more interested in the welfare of someone else rather than themselves.'

'Did someone find out what had happened to Muriel?' Lissa felt guilty that she'd all but forgotten about the missing woman until now.

'Muriel?' Matt frowned and shook his head.

'The wife of the tension pneumothorax,' she reminded him. 'My first patient this evening.'

'Ah, yes!' Matt exclaimed and smiled, shaking his head in apparent bewilderment. 'She was a good case in point. She had a broken leg but she insisted on staying beside one of the other women who was trapped to keep her company until the rescue squad could get to her. Amazing lady. Most of the men I know would have been screaming blue murder and demanding attention for themselves. Is she typically English?'

'Of course,' Lissa said with a smug grin, then added, cheekily, 'She's also typically female. In case you haven't noticed, we're known for being carers and nurturers.'

He conceded the point to her with a laugh, his dark eyes gleaming in spite of the tiredness evident in his face. 'Well, I haven't been nurtured for far too long, and I think it's about time we went and got some coffee.'

'The way my stomach's rumbling, some food would be a good idea, too,' she suggested, wondering at the sudden urge to take care of him. Perhaps it was because her head was too tired to function properly. 'Any idea what time it is?'

'I can't believe it's four o'clock in the morning!' Lissa repeated over her final refill out of an enormous pot of richly aromatic coffee laced with the last of the hot milk and a small spoonful of sugar.

'Five now,' Matt pointed out as he tilted his chair onto its back legs and leant his head lazily against the wall behind him. His hands were wrapped round a matching cereal-bowl-sized cup of the same brew, his own taken black and unsweetened.

They'd started eating an hour ago, she realised in amazement. In spite of the lingering tension from the last few fraught hours and the tiredness natural for the time of night, they certainly hadn't dawdled over the food, both of them far too hungry for anything more than ordinary politeness. Since then they'd remained in the all-but-deserted isolation of the staff canteen and she'd wondered if he was as unwilling as she was to end their time together.

They'd talked about anything and everything, from Taddeo's latest death-defying antics to a comparison of their two countries' health services, and she'd gradually seen the tension ease from his face.

In fact, he looked so relaxed now that she thought he could even be in danger of falling asleep where he sat.

He was slumped almost bonelessly in the chair with his half-closed eyes apparently focused on the dark surface of his coffee and she found herself taking a good long look at him.

She'd only really known him for a few days but his slightly unruly dark hair was already so familiar, looking now as if he'd run his fingers through it more than once. Like that, he looked more like his son than ever.

There were shadows under his eyes that couldn't be camouflaged even by the perennial bronze colour of his skin or the crescents of sinfully long dark lashes. Would the shadows disappear once his workload lightened when the holiday season ended?

She wouldn't be here to find out, she realised with a stab of unexpected regret. She would soon reach the halfway point in her month's holiday, and then it would be time to start thinking about the direction of the rest of her life.

Whatever she decided to do, there certainly wouldn't be time or place in it for ogling gorgeous Italian doctors in the middle of the night, but meanwhile...

Her eyes slid down over the cotton scrubs he'd donned when they'd arrived at the hospital so many hours ago. They were just like the familiar pyjama-style top and trousers she'd first worn during her surgical rotation and had since donned on a daily basis in A and E, impossibly wrinkled-looking even when they were freshly laundered.

Now the wrinkles in Matt's scrubs weren't from the laundry but from use and the fabric was thin enough to delineate almost every one of the muscles she'd last seen exposed on the beach.

She stopped herself from reliving the heart-stopping moment when she'd been lying on her towel to catch her breath after a particularly energetic game of beach volleyball and had felt someone's shadow come between her and the bright warmth of the sun. She had lazily opened her eyes and had looked up...and up the long lean length of bronze thighs and torso to the teasing expression in a pair of gleaming dark eyes.

While she fought to subdue the memory, her eyes had retraced their journey over cotton-covered thighs spread to maintain the angle of the chair against the wall, pausing for several seconds to admire the lean waist doing duty as a table for his coffee, balanced between long lean fingers.

She lingered far longer than she should have on the strangely intimate sight of dark silky-looking hairs framed in the V of the gaping neckline. She knew only too well how thickly they spread across the width of his chest but had no idea what they felt like. If she were to run her fingers through them, would they feel as silky as they looked?

She dragged her eyes and her thoughts away from the tempting prospect and continued upwards to find a darkly knowing pair of eyes waiting for her.

He raised a silent eyebrow and she felt the sudden betraying wash of heat that told her she was blushing.

'I like looking at you, too,' he murmured in a husky voice and her heart gave an extra beat of surprise, but she still couldn't drag her eyes away from his.

How could she have thought he was nearly asleep? She'd never seen his eyes so intent as they were at this moment.

'How is it that you are not married, Melissa?' he asked softly, almost as if he was musing aloud, but the impact of his words was as shocking to her as though he'd doused her with a bucket of ice-cold water.

'Because I'm not. Nor am I likely to be,' she said tersely as the painful memories flooded her mind. She abandoned the last of her coffee without a second glance as she rose to her feet. 'It's late and I'd better be getting back to my hotel. Will there be a taxi outside the hospital or will I have to phone for one?'

'Lissa?' He scrambled rather inelegantly out of his chair and for the first time she found herself looking at him as critically as if he were one of the specimens under the microscope she'd used during her training.

Until now, he'd been the most calm and controlled man she'd ever met, apart from the moment when he'd realised that the injured child she'd cared for had been his son. He was endlessly courteous; considerate even when he was playing games with his son on the beach.

This was the first time she'd seen him caught at a disadvantage and it was almost a relief to find that he was really the same as everyone else.

'I'm sorry, Lissa. What did I say?' he demanded contritely and she was struck by a swift jolt of remorse. It wasn't Matt's fault that through her own poor judgement she'd almost made a monumental mistake. There was no reason to snap at him just because he'd asked a perfectly reasonable question. He wasn't to know that her marital state was a topic she was trying hard to forget, at least for a few more days.

'Nothing, Matt. You didn't do anything. It's just… It's late, and suddenly I'm feeling very tired.'

'Of course. You must be exhausted,' he agreed after an almost imperceptible pause, ushering her towards the door, but there was a new hint of reserve in his tone that told her he hadn't really believed her attempt at evasion.

He politely offered to drive her back to her hotel but when she insisted that a taxi would do just as well, he conceded gracefully. Solicitously, he escorted her into the vehicle and insisted on paying her fare, but she had a feeling that his keenly analytical brain was already working on the enigma of her sudden over-reaction.

How long would it be before he realised that they

might have spoken for several hours today and that he'd told her things about himself that she was certain he'd never told another soul, but that she'd carefully avoided talking about herself at all?

Matt settled himself more comfortably against a buttress of rock and drew in a deep breath of early morning air.

There was something special about being down on the beach so early in the morning, especially when he was the only one there. It seemed almost as if he were the only person left inhabiting a world that had dawned totally fresh and new.

Even after a night without sleep this place had the power to invigorate him...which wasn't a bad thing considering he was due back on duty in just a couple of hours.

He'd probably go in a little early, just to check up on some of the patients they'd treated last night. The fact that no one had needed to bleep him to come in was a good sign. Either there had been no new admissions, or his young junior had been able to cope without him. As for the injured members of the coach party, they were in other hands now. All he could do was hope that his department had done a good enough job on the patients as they'd come in that all they needed was time to recover.

The department had done well, in spite of the sheer weight of numbers, and he had a feeling that their success owed more than a little to the presence of a certain English woman.

Just thinking about her calm confidence was enough to bring her to glorious life in his mind and his pulse rate began to rise.

What *was* this effect she had on him? It wasn't as if

she'd made any effort to flirt with him the way so many others had done over the years. In fact, if he hadn't seen the way she'd been looking at him in the canteen, he would almost have doubted that she'd even noticed he was a man.

Now he had no doubt.

The way her eyes had travelled over his body had made it very hard for him to stay still. It had certainly made it very difficult for him to concentrate his thoughts on something else in a vain attempt at stopping his natural male reaction.

Natural male reaction… He laughed silently. It seemed like a very long time since he'd had a natural male reaction to a female. It must have been several years since the last time he'd even thought about the possibility of taking an attractive woman to his bed. Somehow, the urgency that he'd felt when he'd been younger had completely disappeared once he'd had Taddeo to take care of. In fact, he'd even started to wonder if there might be something amiss…

Well, that was something he didn't need to worry about any more, not since Lissa had appeared in his life. The effect of testosterone overload was back with a vengeance now. He only had to think about the woman to become uncomfortable, and the restraint he had to exercise when he was in her company…

That was probably why he'd found himself talking her ears off yesterday evening. It had seemed like such a good idea to take her to the one place where the sheer weight of memories would outweigh his attraction towards her.

Except it hadn't worked.

She'd seemed to be so genuinely interested in what he'd been telling her, so in tune with what he'd been feeling as he'd relived those distant days, that he'd been more attracted than ever.

Then there had been her appearance; casual rather than model perfect, the breeze tangling her dark curls over her shoulders and around her face with a lover's touch. He'd had to clench his hands into tight fists to subdue the temptation to run his fingers through the glorious strands.

As if that hadn't been enough, she'd been sitting close enough on that rock that, well, he'd *had* to talk. It had been a case of finding some form of distraction or risk losing control and ravishing her on the spot.

He chuckled aloud. *'Svitato!'* As if he was crazy enough to do that! He had far too much respect for her to do such a thing.

But if she were willing…?

He dismissed the voice of temptation with a firm shake of his head.

Yes, she was a beautiful woman and he was a normal man, so of course he would like to take her to bed and make love to her until neither of them could see straight.

But he wasn't going to do it. He wasn't even going to think about it again because the whole idea was impossible. The reservations he'd been carrying about with him for the last five years might have begun to fade since he'd met her but he had far too many responsibilities to contemplate any sort of short-term relationship. It wouldn't be fair to either of them, or to Taddeo. Besides, Lissa was only going to be in the area for a few more weeks.

Yes, he would probably regret his decision, but the regrets would fade. They always did, eventually.

Anyway, apart from that one moment when he'd seen genuine appreciation—maybe even desire—in her eyes, she had certainly done nothing to indicate that she would be interested in any sort of affair.

In fact, she hadn't done or said very much of anything that would let him know about who she was and what she felt.

Now that he thought about it, she actually seemed to be going out of her way to avoid talking about herself in anything but a superficial way.

Did that mean there was some dark secret in her past? Or perhaps it was in her present? Was that why she'd come away to Italy all by herself? Was she yet another woman with a hidden agenda?

The dark cloud of bitter memories started to descend but he refused to allow it.

What did it matter if Lissa *did* have a secret? It was none of his business.

What he had to concentrate on was doing his job to the best of his ability and spending as much time as he could with Taddeo. The time was passing so quickly that already he'd grown beyond that sweet childish stage. Already, he was a little boy and getting more adventurous every day.

A growing cacophony of seabirds drew him out of his contemplation to watch several fishing boats approaching through the brightening day. If the circling, diving throng was anything to go by, they'd had a good catch. Word would spread quickly through San Vittorio and soon there would be an equally noisy throng of people bidding to take the haul home with them.

His solitude broken, Matt glanced down at his watch then turned in the opposite direction to make his way towards the steep steps rather than the gentler zigzag farther along the beach. It wouldn't be long before the sun began to heat the sand, but for now it was cool enough for him to enjoy the feeling of the shifting grains under his bare feet.

It was time to go home and prepare for the day ahead.

Before he went back to the hospital he needed a shower and a shave and a change of clothes and, if he was lucky, he'd have time to drink his first cup of coffee while Taddeo ate his breakfast.

Lissa stepped back out of sight among the rocks and waited until Matt had left the beach.

She felt strangely guilty for watching him like that, almost as if she were some sort of stalker.

'It wasn't as if I'd done it intentionally,' she muttered defensively as she began to make her way slowly towards the noisier end of the beach. But once she'd seen him there, she hadn't been able to resist watching him.

If Matt hadn't laughed aloud she'd never have known he'd been there, leaning against the rocks, but once she'd seen him her heart had leapt into double and triple time.

'Positively juvenile!' she groaned. 'Anyone would think he was a film star or something the way you're reacting.' He was more attractive to her than Leonardo di Caprio. There was nothing of the baby-faced charmer in Matteo Aldarini. He was pure adult male.

His dark trousers had been all but invisible against the shadows of the rocks but his white shirt had gleamed like a beacon even in the strengthening light. It had been unbuttoned to almost halfway down his chest and the fitful breeze was alternately causing it to billow around him then flatten it against his lean body like a second skin.

But it was his face that had caught most of her attention, darkly shadowed by the stubble that had grown since he'd picked her up at the hotel last night. Then, his chin had been so freshly shaven that it had seemed to gleam like polished bronze. Now, with his unruly hair and loose white shirt, the dark shadow along his jaw made him look more like the illustration of a pirate on one of the books she'd seen at the airport than a highly respected doctor.

It was the series of expressions that had crossed his face that intrigued her most. Why *had* he laughed like that? There had been an intriguingly wry note to it. What had he been thinking about? Or was it *who*?

For a moment he'd looked angry, then so sad that she'd ached to go to him and offer comfort.

Before she'd been able to make a fool of herself, intruding where she'd been neither needed nor wanted, he'd been snapped out of his introspection by the arrival of the fishing boats. He'd glanced at his watch and then straightened his shoulders, almost like a soldier preparing to go into battle.

Even as he'd begun to make his way across the sand, his bare feet making him look unexpectedly vulnerable, she'd been tempted to step out of the shadows to greet him in the early morning light. Consideration had had her retreating into the darker hollows.

He'd probably had as little sleep as she had last night, and had obviously come here for a few moments of solitude before he began another busy day. Much as she would have liked to speak to him, she was adult enough to respect his right to privacy and seclusion.

She, on the other hand, was finding that the last thing she wanted was privacy and seclusion. That gave her far too much time in which to pour recrimination down on her own head for the near disaster of her poor judgement.

This trek across the sand was far preferable to sitting in the quiet loneliness of her room.

She'd seen the boats come in most mornings from the window of her room and had decided, this morning, that she would come down and pretend that she was part of the busy scene.

Determined to dwell just on the pleasures of the moment, she drew in a bracing breath of fresh clean air and straightened her shoulders as she looked around.

It was the start of what was obviously going to be yet another beautiful day. Already she could feel the first warmth of the sun as it poured towards her across the Adriatic Sea and not far away there were the busy sounds of energetic haggling going on.

'Forget about him,' she ordered herself as she took off towards the vociferous throng. 'Either he'll be at the hospital today, and far too busy to spare you another thought, or he'll be having a day off and spending it with Taddeo.'

She was close enough now that she might be overheard talking to herself, so she continued the diatribe inside her head.

Whatever he's doing is none of your business. You were able to help out last night only because you've got the necessary skills. As far as being a part of the Aldarinis' extended family circle...that's not even a vague possibility. The only reason you're here is to see where Nonna grew up and to make some decisions about your own future...but not today.

'Hey! Melissa!' called a voice, her name cutting through the cacophony. She was startled. She certainly hadn't expected anyone to recognise her. '*Ciao!* Surely you didn't come here to buy fish?' the voice continued.

A smiling face separated itself from the throng, revealing the familiar figure of Maddelena's mother.

'*Ciao!*' She waved a greeting and went around the edge of the crowd to meet her. 'I'm not buying. I just came out to see what was going on. I can see all this going on each morning from my window.' She gestured over her shoulder towards the hotel.

'Did we wake you up with all our bargaining?' Justina asked with her usual broad smile. 'It's a very Italian thing, to try to get the best price, and for this we have to make a lot of noise, a lot of drama.'

Lissa could see what she meant. If she hadn't known better, the shouting and waving arms would almost have made her believe that war was imminent.

'You didn't wake me. I very rarely sleep during daylight, at least not more than catnaps. I prefer to get an early night to make up on lost sleep.'

'Ah, that must be something to do with your hospital training,' she said sagely. 'Matteo is exactly the same. Sometimes he comes down for a walk on the beach in the morning before he goes to work.'

She glanced over Lissa's shoulder towards the empty expanse of sand and Lissa barely stopped herself from saying, I know.

Far better to feign ignorance, especially since she knew that Matt was already out of sight.

Unfortunately, instead of occupying her mind with other topics, her trip across the sand had just brought the man right back into centre stage. Was she *never* going to be able to think about anything else?

'So, you will come, of course,' Justina was saying with a beaming smile, and Lissa realised that she'd completely missed the conversation.

'*Prego?*' she apologised, hoping she wouldn't have

to explain where her thoughts had been. These days it seemed as if they rarely strayed from one subject.

'*Mi dispiace!* I am so sorry. You are starting to speak Italian so well now that I sometimes forget to speak more slowly.' She patted Lissa's hand. 'I said we are having a party at the weekend. All the family will be coming so you are invited, of course. Shall I give you directions, or shall I ask Matteo to pick you up from the hotel?'

And there she was, her thoughts directed back to the same subject, no matter how hard she struggled. And she knew without trying that there would be no use in attempting to turn down the invitation.

'If you give me directions I can drive myself there— just in case Matt is delayed at the hospital,' she added with a flash of inspiration, loath to spend any more time in the close intimacy of his car. When he was dressed casually he was still the most handsome man she'd ever known. Dressed for a party he would probably be lethal in such close proximity. An overdose, in fact, and she was very much afraid that she had no immunity.

'*Permesso?*' Lissa asked as she stuck her head around the corner of the door to the orthopaedic ward.

She'd managed to last an hour after her walk on the beach before she couldn't bear it any longer. She had to know how 'her' patients were doing.

'*Avanti!*' The sister in charge beckoned with a smile. 'Are you the English doctor my patients have been telling me about? You must be, because you are just the way Dr Aldarini described you.'

CHAPTER FIVE

'Eh, lass, I'm right glad you're 'ere!' a burly man exclaimed in a broad Yorkshire accent. 'I can't make 'ead nor tail of what they're tellin' me, and that's a fact. Why Missus and I 'ad to come on a foreign 'oliday I don't know.'

'So, they've built a Coliseum and a Leaning Tower in Yorkshire, have they?' Lissa countered with a straight face.

'Aye, and put up a giant umbrella to keep the rain out,' chimed in another voice to a chorus of chuckles.

'Nay, tha' knows what I mean,' the first voice interrupted, trying to be heard over the laughter. 'If we'd been in Yorkshire we'd have been on our own doorstep, so to speak.'

'And it's always nicer to be at home if you're feeling ill,' Lissa agreed. 'Still, look on the bright side. You wouldn't have pretty Italian nurses bringing you breakfast in bed if you were in Yorkshire.'

'Not if my wife had anything to do with it, in or out of a plaster cast!' he exclaimed with a roguish twinkle in his eye, then sobered abruptly and beckoned her closer. 'They tell me you saved my life, lass, and I wanted the chance to thank you.'

'No thanks necessary,' she said dismissively, as uncomfortable as ever with praise, then smiled. 'It's all part of the service.'

'What on earth made you decide to come here to work?' called another voice, its owner's legs protected

79

by a cage lifting the bedclothes up in a hump. Lissa found herself wondering if he was one of the people whose lower legs had fractured when he'd been shunted into the seat in front. She'd heard about most of the injuries even if she'd only dealt with a proportion of them personally.

'Aye. Why aren't you working somewhere in England? We're always hearing how much our own hospitals need good doctors,' chimed in another.

'Oh, I don't work here permanently,' Lissa explained quickly. Then she silently added to herself that she didn't really have a job anywhere since she'd worked out her notice. That was one of the things she was going to have to make some decisions about over the next couple of weeks. 'I'm on holiday, too. I just happened to be in the right place at the right time to help out.'

That brought her to the point of her visit.

'Actually, I only called to see if there was anything I could do to help any of you. You know, contact relatives and so on.'

'I'd just like to be able to find out about my wife,' said one voice, and several joined in a chorus of agreement.

'That should be easy enough. I expect the staff here are too busy for too much toing and froing, but my time's my own. Anything else?'

'Could you deliver a message?' asked another.

'No problem. I could even act as a part-time postman, if you like.'

She went from bed to bed around the ward, collecting queries about their own and their loved ones' health. Some she was able to answer immediately but the ward sister was only too willing to supply any details she needed.

'I'm afraid my English is not good enough to explain anything in detail,' she confided quietly when she invited Lissa into her office for a cup of coffee. 'It was very hard to explain to some people that their wives had died. They had no one from their family to cry with them. To be so alone...' She shook her head, her dark eyes glistening with sympathetic tears.

Lissa had been delighted to hear that the prognosis on her first patient was excellent and was quite embarrassed by the praise she'd received for her painstaking stitchery.

'Now I must visit the ladies to deliver these messages,' she said when the phone rang to interrupt their conversation. 'I'll see you later, perhaps.'

'We heard you were coming,' called one woman almost before she'd walked through the door. 'Dr Aldarini promised he wouldn't let you leave without coming in here.'

Just the mention of his name sent a swift surge of warmth up into her face and Lissa swore silently. It was so stupid to react like this. There was absolutely no reason for it. Anyway, how did Matt even know she was in the hospital? She certainly hadn't seen him about.

'I couldn't leave until I'd delivered this stack of messages.' She held up a handful of paper. 'Shall I call out names?'

'If there's one there for me, it'll be the first time he's written to me since he was in the army doing his national service,' quipped one woman.

'Mine's just as bad,' agreed another. 'I probably wouldn't recognise his handwriting any more.'

It was more than an hour before Lissa had visited

them all, having taken the time to say a few words to the Italian patients on her way past.

'Are your people always so cheerful?' demanded one bemused great-grandmother recuperating after a hip replacement. 'They are all injured but they are talking and laughing all the time.'

'Don't tell them I said so,' Lissa murmured in a confidential tone, in spite of the fact that she was speaking in Italian, 'but the people from their region of England are known to be very careful with their money—almost as careful as the people of Scotland. They have all paid good money to come to Italy on holiday and are determined to get their money's worth, even in hospital.'

The elderly woman was still chuckling as Lissa waved goodbye, clutching yet another handful of messages and replies to take in the other direction.

'They've got you running backwards and forwards like a messenger girl,' Matt said with a chuckle as he caught up with her in the corridor. 'Surely you could find better things to do on your holiday?'

Lissa's heart stuttered as she whirled to face him and met those smiling dark eyes.

'I'm only halfway through my stay, so I've still got plenty of time,' she pointed out. 'It hasn't taken very long to sort things out for these people and put their minds at rest.'

'At least it looks as if the rest of them are going to recover from their injuries. We haven't lost any more since the man who had the heart attack last night.'

The poor man had never made it as far as the coronary care unit before he'd died, probably as a result of shock as much as anything else.

'Several were talking about the possibility of being flown home as soon as they're fit to travel. Do you know if there are any procedures to set that in motion?' She was trying hard to keep her mind on her self-imposed task but it was hard when all she wanted to do was savour the man's company.

So much for her determination to keep her distance. At the first opportunity, her stupid heart was turning itself inside out again, and this time it was worse than ever because the man wasn't interested in any sort of long-term relationship.

'I understand that a representative of the tour company came in early this morning to have a word with the hospital administration,' Matt was saying. *He* was obviously having no difficulty in concentrating on the matter in hand. 'Some will probably be able to travel tomorrow if they're admitted into hospital as soon as they arrive in England. Others will have to wait until their injuries are more stable.'

Lissa realised that he was exceptionally well informed about the status of patients who were no longer his responsibility. Staff in A and E departments usually lost track of patients once they were transferred up to wards.

'You came up specially to find out how they all were,' she challenged with a smile, pointing a finger at him.

'So did you,' he countered smugly. 'At least I work here, so I've got an excuse. You're just a visitor who got caught up in it.'

It was a sobering reminder that he belonged here and she didn't, in spite of the fact that she'd felt quite at home to be helping out.

'And I suppose that the fact you're wandering about up here means you haven't enough to do down in the accident department?'

'Oh, there's always plenty to do, but I am allowed time off for good behaviour. Would you like to join me for a cup of coffee?'

In spite of the fact that she'd been given a cup on each ward Lissa found herself agreeing with unseemly haste.

What was it about this man that all her good intentions flew out of the window? It hadn't been that long ago that she'd decided to keep men out of her life for the foreseeable future, but all Matteo Aldarini had to do was extend an invitation and she couldn't wait to accept.

What did she know about the man, for heaven's sake, apart from the fact that he was handsome and sexy enough to have every one of her hormones in turmoil?

She knew that he had no family, apart from his son, and that he was a doctor in the hospital's emergency department and his grandfather had once taken him to see a wolf. It wasn't really enough for her to be swamped by such a strong attraction towards him.

She'd been attracted to other men…well, to one man in particular… A man with whom she'd seemed to have had so much in common that she'd even been planning to spend the rest of her life with him…until she'd found out that nothing was what it seemed.

If that episode had taught her anything, it was that she had appalling instincts where suitable men were concerned.

Still, she was only here for another couple of weeks, so nothing could go wrong.

She was attracted to him and there was nothing untoward in that. He was such a good-looking man that he probably had half the staff of the hospital panting after him. And after that heated gaze they'd shared just a few hours ago, she knew that he was attracted to her, too, for all the good it would do them.

It was flattering to find herself the object of his interest, but if they were to act upon it, the only possible outcome would be disaster.

One of those was enough heartache in one lifetime.

'You can't seem to stay away from us,' teased Matt as he brought over a tray containing not just the promised coffee but something that looked suspiciously like spaghetti carbonara as well. 'Are you a workaholic or is your holiday not working out as well as you'd anticipated?'

'I wouldn't say I was a workaholic, although I do enjoy my work,' she responded, taking his question seriously. 'It took me a long time to decide what branch of medicine I wanted to specialise in.'

'What other fields did you consider?' He was clearly interested.

'Surgery, first,' she said and saw him blink in surprise.

'Not a popular choice for women,' he commented, as if he was being careful of his words. 'Especially if you were going for general surgery rather than something more 'lightweight' such as cosmetic or paediatric.'

'Lack of upper body strength is always a problem for women,' she agreed. 'I realised that the first time I observed the sheer brute force needed to do a successful hip replacement. Then there's the number of years it takes to train as a surgeon. It can take almost a third of your working life to climb your way to the top.'

'So you chose emergency medicine instead. Was that because it's such a low-stress environment?' he teased.

'Ha! You know as well as I do that it can go from nothing to manic in the time it takes for the doors to open. And you rarely have time to breathe, let alone ask someone for a second opinion.'

'So why do it?' He'd paused with a forkful of carbonara halfway to his mouth, his eyes very intent on her face as if he really wanted to know what she thought. 'Wouldn't it be an easier life if you decided to go into general practice? You would certainly have more time for a social life…a family, perhaps?'

Lissa grew still. Matt's words were an uncomfortable echo of another time and another place. Someone else had wanted her to choose a direction that would take her to a comfortable life with predictable hours.

'I thought about it,' she admitted and deliberately put a dismissive tone in her voice. 'But I decided that, in spite of the relatively high burn-out rate of emergency physicians, that was the work I wanted to do.'

'Front-line medicine?' He lifted one dark eyebrow in an almost challenging expression.

'If you like. It's certainly one in which you know almost immediately if you've made the right diagnosis and chosen the right treatment.'

'As with that tension pneumothorax,' he agreed with an approving smile that warmed her deep inside. 'A perfect diagnosis followed by a perfect technique to remedy it, and your embroidery isn't bad either. That was some very neat work on those lacerations.'

Lissa was glad that he'd lightened the atmosphere. She'd grown unaccustomed to holding such intense conversations over the last few months. At one time she'd been just as likely as any other young doctor to expound at length on any number of subjects. Her brief time as the cynosure of the hospital grapevine had made her wary of drawing attention to herself.

'Thank you for your kind words. I'm just glad I was able to help.'

'You seem to be doing that a lot around here. I don't know what you must be thinking about the medical services in this region.'

'It's probably no better and no worse than any comparable region in my own country. We have areas that suffer a massive influx of holiday visitors that leave the emergency services impossibly stretched. But, just like yours, they're staffed by excellent doctors and nurses who do the best they can with what they've got. I don't think anyone can ask more.'

'Do *you* work in such an area or are you based in a city?' he asked.

Lissa's heart gave an uncomfortable thud. It was the first direct question he'd asked that she really hadn't wanted to answer. It skirted far too close to things she'd rather not think about yet. Unfortunately there wasn't any real way of avoiding an answer.

'My last post was in a city hospital accident and emergency department,' she said quietly, facing him straight on and waiting for a response, knowing that he was too intelligent not to pick up on the way she'd phrased it.

'Was?' That eyebrow had gone up again before a frown pleated his forehead.

'I worked out my notice just before I came away. I'll be looking for a new job when I return to England.'

He was obviously waiting for her to explain, but it was beyond her. There was no way she could tell him what had led to the handing in of her resignation without going into all the details of her disastrous lack of judgement.

'How about applying for a job in Italy?' he suggested out of the blue, and took her breath away.

'What?' she gasped, then laughed in disbelief. 'I couldn't do that!'

'Why not?' he countered, his calm voice strangely at odds with his intent expression. 'We've already formally verified your credentials. So we could give you a formal offer of a post—you'd only need a work permit and a residence permit and they're both available from the police station.'

'But—' It was like trying to stop a runaway train with a feather for all the effect it had on him.

'You've seen first hand how badly stretched we get if there's only *one* serious problem arriving on our doorstep, but even on an ordinary day the accident department is kept hopping. We've been trying to get another doctor for the department for some time so you wouldn't be taking a job away from an Italian national. What's more, you've actually trained specifically for the job, so you would be perfect.'

'Matt…stop!' She finally got a word in edgeways. 'You don't even know me. You certainly don't know much about my past career or my level of expertise. For all you know I could be a…a…' She was lost for words.

'A mass murderer? I don't think so. Not the person who took so much care to protect the back and neck of a stranger's child in case he'd injured his spine. Not the person who insisted on coming in to help out with the victims of that coach crash. Not the person who came in the next day to visit her countrymen and -women just in case she could do something to help them.'

'Oh, Matt, you're impossible. The whole idea's crazy. I couldn't possibly—'

'Don't say no,' he ordered. 'Promise me you'll at least think about it.'

'But, Matt—'

'Please. Say you'll think about it,' he repeated insistently. 'It's a good job in a beautiful place with wonderful people. How can you possibly turn it down? Someone as beautiful as you will fit in perfectly. Why wouldn't I try to persuade you to stay?' His final flirtatious words made it sound as if he was teasing, but Lissa was suddenly aware that there was something far more serious going on under the surface.

Was he really so desperate to ease the burden on his staff that he would try anything to recruit another doctor? Even outrageous flattery? He'd certainly been at the end of his rope the first time they'd met.

Whatever his reason, at least she knew that the strange intensity she was picking up on was unlikely to be because he really wanted *her* to take the job. He'd made his initial interest in her quite plain within a very short time of meeting her, and when she'd opted for a simple friendship he'd accepted almost ridiculously easily—almost as if it didn't matter much to him one way or the other. After all, a good-looking man like him wouldn't lack for women willing to accept his invitations to…whatever.

It was a good job she didn't have a tender ego to protect, she thought wryly. That was one thing she'd had to get rid of in a hurry when her bad judgement had been revealed.

'It's a good job I was warned that flirting is practically an obligatory ritual for the Italian male,' she teased, shaking her head. 'Nonna said it's even more prevalent here in the South, where the problems faced by women are closely linked to the problems of Italian men.'

'What do you mean, the "problems" of Italian men?' he demanded. That had clearly stung his male ego.

'Well, there's the traditional Italian adoration of the male child that often continues right into adulthood. Far too many of them live at home until they're in their thirties, with their mothers running around after them as if they were some sort of god. Then they expect their wives to continue like that when they marry.'

'They're out of luck these days, then,' Matt commented dryly. 'The statistics show that fewer and fewer women are going out looking for Mr Right. They now seem to prefer the freedom of making their own way in life. And as for staying home to pander to the whims of husband and son when they *do* marry, most say they want to keep their jobs instead of having children at all.'

'So the traditional Italian family that extends to dozens of cousins is becoming a thing of the past?' Lissa was sure she'd heard something about Italy's falling birth rate before. She vaguely remembered that for the first time the population was actually declining rather than increasing because the young were either choosing not to marry or, if they did choose a partner, were deciding not to have large families.

'We could end up with the same problem as they're discovering in China,' he continued. 'With the law restricting each family to one child, the children are being spoiled to death.'

'Uh-oh! Not another race of men like the Italians,' Lissa teased. 'Can the world cope with two races who spoil their men so dreadfully that they think they're God's gift to women?'

'We're not *so* bad,' he objected with a frown. 'Anyway, what's so wrong with telling women that we find them attractive and desirable? I would have thought that they would be pleased.'

There was nothing wrong with his choice of words. They could have been overheard by anyone without raising an eyebrow. It was the expression she saw in his eyes that sent a surge of heated awareness right through her.

He might have been talking in generalisations, but the way he looked at her implied very clearly that he was talking about her.

Was he?

Did he really mean that he found her attractive and desirable or was this just another example of his flirtatious nature at work?

She was just wondering if she dared to challenge him when she heard his name in amongst the flood of Italian issuing from a nearby speaker.

'Problem?' she asked when he groaned in response.

'Only another group of people apparently struck down with some bug.' He murmured an apology and strode across to the in-house phone.

Lissa made use of the time to clear the remains of their meal onto the tray. She hovered for a moment, not quite certain what to do. It was hardly polite to walk across to join him when he was in the middle of a call, but neither was it polite to leave without thanking him for buying her meal.

The dilemma was solved when he turned to beckon her to his side.

'I don't suppose you've got an afternoon free?' he said with a roguish lift of an eyebrow. 'It sounds like another case of food poisoning coming in, but this time it's a wedding reception involved.'

The words 'wedding reception' were enough to send a sinking sensation through her, but there were more important things to think about than her own misfortune.

'How many involved?' she demanded as she followed him out into the corridor, turning as if by rote in the right direction to find the nearest bank of lifts.

On the periphery of her mind she noted that she hadn't even bothered to answer his initial question, nor had he waited for her to agree to help out. It was almost as though she had already accepted a post on the hospital staff and was merely being asked to stay on for some voluntary overtime.

The feeling was slightly unnerving.

The sight that met them when they reached the emergency department was uncomfortably similar to the one she'd seen the first time that she'd walked through the doors. The main difference this time was the fact that every one of their patients was dressed in their smartest or prettiest clothes as befitted guests at an upscale wedding.

A sudden flash of white at the other side of the reception area drew her eyes and she realised that even the bride and groom were in attendance.

'*Che disastro!*' exclaimed the senior nurse as she hurried past the two of them with a stack of disposable kidney dishes.

'Where do you want me first?' Lissa offered. 'Which end of the age scale?' The frailer members of the party would be the most likely to suffer serious ill effects if they started to become dehydrated, and that meant the youngest children and the grandparents and great-grandparents.

'Would you start with the littlest ones?' he directed. 'Most of their parents will have more of a grasp of modern medicine and English if you get into difficulties. When the older ones get sick they can sometimes panic and become irrational. The idea of being attended to by a ''foreign'' doctor might be the last straw.'

The senior nurse had obviously drawn the same conclusion as, without having to say a word, Lissa found herself directed into the first cubicle and found a very miserable three-year-old waiting for her.

'Is she going to die? Please, don't let her die,' begged her distraught mother over the sound of her daughter's screams. The only pause in the noise came when the little mite's stomach made another attempt at ridding itself of the infected food, most of the evidence now smeared right down the front of her beautiful pale pink lace dress.

'She's too noisy to die,' Lissa said into one brief lull and startled both parents into a watery chuckle. 'But she's being very sick and we will need to give her fluids so she doesn't become dehydrated. This will help her body to get rid of the toxins making her ill.'

'Can you give her something to stop her being sick?' pleaded her mother. 'I can't bear to see her so ill.'

'I'll find out if we've got something suitable for a little body. Can you tell me how old she is and how much she weighs so we can work out a dose?'

While she kept them talking her hands were busy with the tray handed to her by a young nurse. Almost before the youngster realised what was happening there was a needle in her arm carefully disguised under the bright blue bandage holding it to a splint. All that was visible was a thin plastic pipe delivering the clear fluid dripping down from the IV bag.

It was a simple matter to add the carefully calibrated dose of antiemetic to the fluid entering her arm.

'Just give her a cuddle until she's feeling better,' Lissa advised the mother gently then turned to the rather grey-looking father standing helplessly by while everything went on around him.

'I think your wife probably needs a cuddle, too,' she suggested, not daring to say that he looked as if he could do with one as well. Still, the act of giving his wife comfort should satisfy the 'take charge' side of his masculinity.

That was none of her concern, though. There were plenty of patients waiting to be seen, the next one in the adjoining cubicle.

'How is it going?' Matt asked some two hours later when they finally stopped long enough to draw breath.

'Well, all I can say is you certainly lay on a good test to see if your potential doctors are up to the job!' she teased wearily. 'Of course, it could have the opposite effect and send them screaming all the way back to the city.'

'How about if I were to offer you a cup of coffee, complete with frothy milk and sugar, just the way you like it, and specially prepared with my own two hands?' he suggested with a roguish smile. 'Would that make you think better of the situation?'

CHAPTER SIX

'THAT was a truly dreadful afternoon,' Matt announced as he sprawled back in his chair and groaned.

'I don't think I'll want to eat for a week,' Lissa agreed, trying to forget just how many sick people they'd had to deal with.

'At least, not at *that* restaurant,' he added slyly, and she nearly choked on her coffee.

'Well, one good thing has come out of it,' she pointed out when she had herself under control again. 'We've discovered that the restaurant where the wedding reception was being held was part of the same hotel where your last food-poisoning victims were staying, so that has narrowed the search for a common cause down a bit.'

'You're right. For a while I was beginning to wonder if we'd got some sort of water-borne infection in the San Vittorio area. *E. coli*, perhaps. That would have been a total disaster for the tourist trade, never mind the health of the local residents. At least we now know that the problem is limited to one establishment.'

'I would hate to see what happens to the restaurant's insurance premiums when the bridal party sues for compensation for a ruined wedding reception,' Lissa said with a grimace. 'To say nothing about the number of people who are going to have to stay in hospital until they're strong enough to go home.'

'How can any amount of money replace the bad memories of today?' Matt argued. 'Her wedding day is supposed to be the happiest day of a woman's life, isn't it? Even if the hotel were to supply that couple with another reception at a later date, it would never be the same.'

'What do you mean, the happiest day of a *woman's* life?' Lissa challenged, deliberately concentrating on being contentious rather than allowing herself to dwell on the abandoned might-have-beens in her own life. 'That's a very sexist remark. Don't you think the man might be just as happy to be marrying the woman he loves?'

Matt seemed almost startled by her words and was silent for a moment, the expression in his eyes very analytical as they met hers. 'Sometimes, I wonder,' he admitted slowly, softly, almost as if he wasn't aware that he was speaking aloud.

Lissa had a strange feeling that something momentous was going on inside that clever head.

What had he meant? Did he wonder whether a man could be just as happy as a woman, or was it more basic than that? Was he wondering whether there was such a thing as a happy marriage?

Perhaps if she knew what had happened to Taddeo's mother, she might be closer to understanding, but all the while she was reluctant to talk about her own secrets, she could hardly presume to ask Matt to talk about his.

'Well, at least I've got some time off coming up in a couple of days,' he said suddenly, almost leaping to his feet as though to escape his thoughts. 'Anything special planned then, or would you like to come on a trip?'

'A trip?' The suggestion was completely unexpected, especially after he'd been sunk in such deep thoughts.

He wasn't really inviting her to go away with him, was he? Her heart rate doubled in an instant.

'With Taddeo, of course,' he added as though that was an extra incentive, and her spirits took a stupid dive. Of course he wasn't inviting her away on an intimate trip for two with him. She already knew that he wasn't looking for any sort of permanence otherwise he would be married already. With Taddeo along, her place was obviously as nothing more than a pleasant companion, which was exactly what she had told him she wanted to be.

So why was she feeling so disappointed?

Confused by the mixed feelings whirling around inside her, she couldn't decide what to say, in spite of the almost eager expression she'd glimpsed.

At her hesitation his face became suddenly blank, but he couldn't hide the fact that there was turmoil going on behind those dark eyes.

'Lissa, I'm sorry if I presumed...' he began, then stopped as though lost for words.

He hesitated a moment and then perched on the edge of the seat nearest to her, leaning forwards to brace his elbows on his knees. He linked his fingers into a cat's cradle and stared down at them in silence and she knew he was trying to decide what to say.

She was mystified. This wasn't like Matt. He wasn't a hesitant man. He was decisive and forthright and...

'After our outing the other evening I started thinking about my grandfather,' he began quietly, startling her out of her thoughts with the slightly rusty tone of his voice and the unexpected direction of his conversation.

'It was probably the fact that I'd told you about him that brought him to mind so clearly, but the thing that stuck in my memory was his sympathy with the wolves.'

He glanced briefly at her, almost as though he needed the reassurance that she was still listening, that she was interested.

She couldn't drag her eyes away, the glimpse of what he'd been like as a little boy coming across very clearly in that moment and tugging at her heartstrings. He was so uncannily like Taddeo that, under other circumstances, it would have been amusing.

'I've been haunted by the fact that, with my grandfather and my parents gone, there are just the two of us left. That means it's up to me to tell my son about our family heritage or it will be lost for ever.' He sighed heavily, his shoulders slumping with something more than mere tiredness after a busy shift.

'Then there's the fact that the numbers of wolves have gone down so much since I was five that I will probably never be able to recreate that magical night up in the mountains for him.'

She remembered clearly the echo of that childhood fascination in the man's voice and the fact that it had never left him, and understood only too well what he meant. He'd captured her imagination with his tale of that long-ago sighting so that she couldn't wait to see a wolf for herself.

'So, in two days' time we're setting off early to drive up to the Abruzzo National Park to see the wolves. Oh, I know it's not the same,' he continued hurriedly when she would have spoken, one hand held up to halt her interruption. 'They've been rounded up, enclosed within the boundaries of the park and demystified into a tourist attraction, but even so, I thought you might...' He shrugged, almost as though apologising for his burst of fervour.

'I would love to come with you,' Lissa said quietly, her heart suddenly strangely full at the thought that he genuinely wanted her with them. Over the last few days she'd sometimes had the feeling that he wasn't quite happy about his son spending so much time with her. Obviously she'd been wrong.

'I know you're on holiday but can you be ready by seven?' he asked with a return of that wicked gleam in his eye.

'I'm a doctor. I can be ready whatever time I set my alarm for. You ought to know that,' she pointed out huffily, fighting back an answering grin as she stuck a disdainful nose in the air. 'Anyway, I'm not very likely to sleep past seven with the boats bringing their catch in, am I?'

'I stand corrected.' He suited his actions to his words and bowed in her direction. 'If the *signorina* has finished with her coffee, her carriage awaits. I've got a full day's work to do tomorrow before I can take time off to play.'

It was still quite dark when Lissa made her way down to the beach two days later.

She hadn't needed to set her alarm to remind herself to get up. In fact, it seemed as if she'd hardly slept for two nights for the electric anticipation humming along every nerve.

She'd even been distracted during yesterday's visit to the remaining coach-crash victims, imagining she could hear Matt's voice around every corner. It had been a good job that some of the relatives had arrived to keep the convalescents entertained because she'd done a poor job of it.

This morning was no better.

She'd been up and dressed for hours, padding barefoot round her hotel room, unable to settle to anything. Finally, with a sympathetic thought for the people trying to sleep in the rooms adjoining hers, she'd been driven to seek distraction outside.

'Get a grip on yourself,' she muttered as she made her way barefoot towards the hard-packed sand at the water's edge. She paused to roll up the bottoms of her jeans then stepped into the lacy edge of the waves and let them swirl around her ankles.

'It's no big deal,' she declared into the darkness as she felt the water swirl the sand away from around her toes. She gazed along the edge of the beach and watched the way the lights of the buildings closest to the beach caught the frothy edges of the waves. Slowly she made her way along the wavering line, hoping the rhythmic ebb and flow would calm her down.

'It's only a day's outing with his son to show him some wolves,' she reminded herself sternly. 'It's not as if it's the start of a relationship…but, then, you're not in the market for a relationship, anyway.'

Even over the susurration of the waves she could hear snatches of her words eddying around her and the bare truth in them brought her down to earth with a bump.

What on earth did she think she was doing?

It might only be an innocent outing with Matt and his son but for some strange reason it had started to feel like so much more. And she certainly couldn't afford to take the risk that it might start to develop into anything important.

It wasn't so very long ago that she'd had her heart

shredded and her trust destroyed. It was going to be years before she was ready to risk that sort of pain again.

So what was she doing, agreeing to spend the day with Matteo Aldarini, even if his little son was going to be there with them?

The man was too good-looking and far too sexy for her peace of mind, to say nothing of the fact that he was a genuinely nice person, an excellent doctor and a caring parent. In fact, he was everything that she'd thought she'd found when she'd fallen in love with...

Lissa closed her eyes, her teeth clenched tightly as she forced the hurtful memories back into their deep dark corner.

'Just poor judgement,' she muttered. 'Nothing fatal. It's not as if I'd made a clinical error and administered a lethal dose of a drug.' Except that the effects had felt pretty deadly at the time.

When she'd met him she'd started thinking about for ever and happily-ever-after but all her plans had collapsed like a flimsy house of cards.

And if she spent too much time with Matt, she was very much afraid she would be setting herself up for heartache all over again.

It was all very well to keep reminding herself that she'd sworn to keep her distance, but if she was honest with herself she would have to admit that it was becoming more and more difficult.

At first she'd only been affected by Matt's charisma when she was in his company but now she didn't even have to be near him to feel herself respond to the thought of him.

'Keep it cool, I've been telling myself. Keep your distance. Ha!' she scoffed and flung her hands up in the air. 'If it was that easy I'd still be sleeping like a baby, not marching up and down the beach at stupid-o'clock in the morning because I can't wait to see him.'

The sky had slowly begun to lighten while she was berating herself and she saw that she'd reached the little niche where she'd caught sight of Matt the other morning.

Feeling more than a little foolish, she stepped across the sand to settle herself in the same place, closing her eyes as she leant her head back against the wave-sculpted rock.

'Time for some serious thought,' she whispered and took silent stock of her facts.

Two weeks ago she hadn't even known of Matt's existence. If she hadn't stepped in to take care of Taddeo on this very beach she'd probably never have met him.

So what, if he was a handsome man. There were millions of handsome men in the world.

'But none of the others make my heart beat faster,' she heard herself admit. 'None of the others make a tiny piece of my heart brave enough to feel that it just might be worth taking a chance on him.'

She sighed and shook her head in despair.

How stupid could she be? There were only another two weeks to her holiday and then she had to return to the real world. She was going to be thrown into a frenzy of job interviews and flat-hunting almost as soon as her plane landed, with not a second spare to mope about a holiday romance gone wrong.

It had been bad enough coping with the aftermath of one disaster in her life. Did she really want another?

A faint sound intruded on her thoughts, slowly growing until she recognised the rhythmic chugging sound of the engines of the incoming fishing boats.

'What time is it?' she gasped, her eyes flying to her watch. 'Five minutes to seven!'

Where had the time gone? she wondered as her feet flew across the sand, heading for the closest steps leading up towards the hotel. If she didn't hurry, she was going to be late.

She was almost breathless by the time she'd run all the way up the stairs to her room, unwilling to wait even a moment for the lift. She tried to tell herself that it was because she didn't want to keep Matt and Taddeo waiting. In her heart of hearts she had to admit that the real reason why she didn't want to be late was that she didn't want to waste a single second of her day with Matt.

'Punctual to the second,' Matt said with a teasing smile as he accelerated the car away from the front of the hotel. 'I like that in a woman.'

Lissa tried to act offended but her heart was still beating out the tattoo of delight that had started when she'd first caught sight of him and all she could do was send him an answering smile.

It wasn't fair that he could look just as devastating in a pair of jeans and a casual shirt as he did in a suit and tie. Nor was it fair that the sight robbed her of the power of rational thought.

All she could think was that she was pleased to see him and pleased to be spending the day with him, but she wouldn't be admitting to that. And she certainly wouldn't be telling him that her brain was so scrambled by the thought of spending time in his company that she'd just been racing round her room like a madwoman, looking for her missing shoes. It was only when she'd tried to fling her hands up in the air in exasperation that she'd discovered that she was carrying them around in her hand.

'We're going for a surprise,' announced a little voice from the back seat and she turned to peer around her headrest. The sight of Taddeo wearing a miniature version of his father's outfit with an array of toys and books scattered on either side of his securely belted body was enough to loosen her tongue.

'Are we, *girino*?' She'd been using the Italian word for tadpole as his nickname for over a week now, and he giggled every time. 'What's the surprise?'

'We don't know, or it wouldn't be a surprise,' he explained with patient logic. 'But *Papà* said we have to drive for a long time to get there. It's up in the mountains called…'

'Abruzzo,' his father supplied when Taddeo ground to a halt.

'That's right. The 'bruzzo mountains and there's a special sort of a park there where people can't build houses and factories so there's still room for all the birds and animals and trees.'

'Conservation theory in a nutshell,' Matt muttered in an aside and Lissa had to hide a grin. It was just such a good feeling to be able to share that sort of remark with him. It was almost as if they were an ordinary couple taking off for the day with their child.

Dangerous thoughts. Far too dangerous if she wanted to avoid heartbreak.

'So, what do you think we're going to see? Elephants?' she suggested brightly.

'Elephants don't live in Italy!' Taddeo exclaimed in a scandalised voice. 'Only in a zoo.'

'What about whales?' his father offered, quick to join in the game. 'Do you think we're going to see whales?'

'No! They don't live in the mountains,' his son objected with an infectious giggle. 'They live in an ocean. I know…how about dinosaurs? You know, *Papà*, like we saw in that film.'

'Were they in Italy? In the Abruzzo Mountains?' Matt challenged.

'No. In America, I think,' Taddeo answered with a thoughtfulness far beyond his years. 'Only not really. It was just a film because all the really big dinosaurs are dead.'

'So there are still some little dinosaurs around, are there?' Lissa posed, interested to find out what he'd say.

'Not exactly,' he answered seriously. 'But some animals were alive at the same time as the dinosaurs.'

'Do you know which ones?' Matt asked, the glance he threw at Lissa so full of pride in his son that her throat tightened.

What must it be like to listen to your child having such an adult conversation? Would she ever know what it felt like?

'Well, there's lizards and tortoises and some sorts of beetles…and there's some plants and trees, too. I could show you in one of my books, if you want. When we go back home.'

Mention of his books reminded him of the selection he'd brought with him and left Lissa free to face forwards again.

'He's a very bright boy,' she murmured so that only Matt would hear. 'And a very loveable one. You're doing a good job of bringing him up on your own.'

'I can't take all the credit because I'm not doing it alone. My job is a full-time one, as you can understand.

I couldn't have managed without Maddelena and her family.'

'What about Taddeo's mother?'

The question slipped out before she could stop it and hung in the air between them like a small poisonous cloud.

She knew she shouldn't have asked, but the missing woman had been on her mind more and more until she couldn't bear it any longer. Matt had said he wasn't married and that Taddeo didn't have a mother, but...

'His mother is dead, of a drugs overdose,' Matt said bluntly and it wasn't until the shock of his words began to sink in that she realised he had switched out of his own language into hers so that Taddeo couldn't overhear.

'Does he know?' Her heart ached for both of them, the motherless child and the man who had loved her enough to give her that child.

'He's been told that his mother's gone to heaven, but he's never really missed her because she'd never cared for him.'

'Never...?' she repeated on a soft gasp. How could any woman not want to care for such a wonderful little boy?

'He was just a means to an end, but then, when the pregnancy didn't achieve what she wanted it to, she just abandoned him.' He was speaking softly but even so she could hear cold steel in his tone.

She dared a glance in his direction and found that his expression matched his voice. A shiver ran the length of her spine in response and she hoped she never had that tone directed at her.

He was silent for a moment, staring out through the windscreen with his hands clenched so tightly around the steering-wheel that his knuckles showed bone white against the bronze of his skin.

Lissa was convinced that he'd said as much as he was going to when he broke the silence again.

'We met at a fashion show that was staged as a fund-raiser for the hospital and I was attracted to her. Hell, every man in the room was attracted to her, but for some reason she made a play for me.'

He sounded surprised but Lissa wasn't. She could understand any female from six to sixty wanting to make a play for him, let alone a top-flight fashion model.

'She tricked me,' he said suddenly, almost forgetting to keep his voice low. 'Deceived me into making her pregnant because her boyfriend couldn't father a child.'

Lissa was so shocked that there was nothing she could say. That didn't mean that the pain she could hear in his voice wasn't having an effect on her. All she wanted to do was wrap him in her arms as if he were no older than his little son.

'What she didn't find out until too late was that the reason why her boyfriend couldn't father a child was because he didn't *want* one. He'd deliberately had a vasectomy to make certain.'

'But…' She paused. There were too many questions she wanted to ask, and none of the answers were any of her business.

'You might as well know the whole thing,' he grated, self-reproach clear in every word. 'She was a model, a very beautiful one who was afraid of growing old. She admitted, after she was certain she was pregnant, that she'd been living with a man who was a highly sought-after fashion photographer, but she was desperate for security.'

Probably out of habit he'd been very careful not to mention names but Lissa wasn't really interested in finding out who he was talking about, just about how their actions had affected Matt and Taddeo.

'So she thought that if she had his child… But it wasn't his child.' She shook her head, totally confused.

'I don't really know what her reasoning was,' he admitted. 'Whether she'd hoped to fool him into believing the child was his, or if she'd hoped he would be so delighted at the unexpected chance to be a father.' He shook his head. 'The minute he found out she was pregnant he told her that she was finished. With him and with her career.'

'And she came back to you?' It was a question, but she already knew the answer.

'No matter what she'd done, or why, it was my child,' he said simply, just as she'd known he would. 'When the pregnancy was over she spent a month working night and day to get her figure back then tried to see the guy again. He wouldn't even return her calls.'

'And that's when she…'

He sighed deeply. 'You can't help hearing about the lengths some models will go to in their quest to be thinner—endless hours of exercise, crazy diets. Far too many of them end up resorting to drugs to suppress their appetite, even hard drugs. Apparently she went out one night and bought all she could afford and took it all in one go. She'd been dead for over twelve hours before the friend she'd been staying with woke up and found her.'

'What a waste,' Lissa whispered sadly.

'Are we nearly there, yet, *Papà*?' demanded a little voice from the back and they were both instantly dragged back to the normality of the present moment.

'Not yet, but if you can wait until we reach the next service area we could stop for a while to have a drink and something to eat,' Matt offered and his voice sounded surprisingly level.

Lissa wasn't certain she could have recovered her poise so fast and found herself distractedly agreeing that they all needed a break in their journey. Even though she'd been up so early her stomach had been too full of butterflies to contemplate breakfast.

They had pulled into a parking bay in the next service area and were releasing their seat belts when they heard an electronic bleeping.

'That's *not* your hospital pager!' Lissa exclaimed in surprise and disappointment. 'You said you're off duty today.'

'It's not my pager. That wouldn't work this far away. It's my mobile phone.' Matt turned round in his seat to fish it out of the pocket in the jacket he'd thrown in the corner beside Taddeo.

She heard him curse softly when he saw the number revealed on the display and had a nasty feeling that their beautiful day was about to be spoiled.

'*Pronto!*' he barked with a fierce frown then fell silent.

Lissa had no idea who was on the other end but she could certainly tell that they were upset.

'*Calmarsi!*' he exclaimed in a very different voice. '*Maddelena, calmarsi!*' He was infinitely soothing, obviously needing to get her to calm down before he could make sense of a word she was saying.

By the time he ended the call Lissa had a good idea what had happened and knew that their trip was all but over.

'Justina…Maddelena's mother…has had a bad fall,'

he announced tersely, confirming her suspicions. 'It's very likely that she has broken her hip and her husband is away at the moment on a conference.' He turned to look at Taddeo, speaking to him directly as though he were another adult. 'I'm sorry we aren't going to be able to finish our trip today, but Maddelena's mother is hurt and we must go back to look after her.'

Taddeo looked stricken. 'She's not going to die, is she?' he blurted, his little face quite pinched and white.

'No, *caro*. Of course she's not going to die, but she's going to need our help because she's going to have to stay in the hospital until her leg is feeling better.'

'Is Lissa going to help us? She's a doctor, too,' he pointed out earnestly.

'Of course I'll help, if your *papà* wants me to,' she promised and turned to open her door. 'Now, I'm just going to go to the shop to get us some juice to drink and something to eat while the two of you stretch your legs. Then we can start the journey back.'

When it seemed as if Matt would question the delay she gestured towards the block of toilets and raised a significant eyebrow in Taddeo's direction.

'Good idea,' he agreed with a nod. 'We'll meet you back here.'

The sun was fiercely hot after the comfort of the air-conditioned car but Lissa barely noticed as she made her way swiftly across the car park and into the service area.

When she had her emotions under control she knew that she would understand Matt's need to return to help Justina in any way he could, but at the moment all she could feel was a crushing sense of disappointment.

This was all happening far too soon after their conversation about Taddeo's mother. She was afraid that cutting short their day after such a fraught subject might leave Matt feeling uncomfortable in her company. He'd certainly revealed far more about his private torment than she'd ever expected and she was afraid that it might be enough to make him avoid her from now on.

The rational side of her mind knew that this would probably be the best thing, in the circumstances, but her emotional side couldn't bear the thought that this might be the last time they spent together.

CHAPTER SEVEN

'LISSA, may I ask you a favour?' Matt said quietly, breaking a silence that had gone on for over an hour.

After a quick phone call to the hospital to confirm that Justina was in good hands, he'd decided that they could afford to take long enough for a proper breakfast.

Since then, apart from a brief flurry of questions from Taddeo about what was happening to his honorary aunt, they'd all been immersed in their own thoughts.

'A favour?' She had no idea what she could possibly do for him.

'Well, I won't be able to take Taddeo into the hospital with me, and I can't ask Maddelena to come out and look after him. She'll want to be with her mother.'

Lissa smiled wholeheartedly. 'So you'd like me to keep him company? Of course I will, if he doesn't mind.' She turned to look around the headrest at him. 'What do you say, *girino*? Will you be my guide while we do a bit of sightseeing? Perhaps a bit of shopping?'

'Will it be boring shopping?' he asked with a frown that was a perfect miniature of his father's.

'Only if you take me to boring shops,' she promised. He grinned.

'OK! No boring shops. *Papà*, where is that *very* expensive toy shop you wouldn't take me in? And I remember how to find the shop that has computer games that you can try out before you buy them, and—'

'You might regret this, if you live that long,' Matt warned with a twinkle in his eyes.

'No way!' she exclaimed. 'I've been wanting to have a go at some of those games for ages. I saw some of them up in the paediatric department at my old job, but the kids would never stop playing long enough for me to try.'

Matt rolled his eyes and pulled a face that set both Lissa and Taddeo laughing.

'Am I the only adult in this car?' he demanded in mock despair as he guided the car through the snarl of traffic in the old-fashioned centre of San Vittorio.

'Yeah!' his son jeered. 'Too old to have fun on computers!'

'Cheeky wretch! Just you wait till I get you home!' Matt threatened to the sound of his son's renewed giggles. 'So, where shall I drop you off? Are you going to start off in the toy shop and finish up with the computers?'

'Sounds like a good plan,' she agreed. 'What do you think, *girino*?'

'Great! Then we can play with all the computer games until *Papà*'s finished at the hospital.'

'At least I'll know where to find you,' he said wryly as he pulled over to the kerb. 'I shouldn't be more than an hour or so, but if I'm any longer you can always take a taxi to the hospital.'

'We'll be fine, Matt. Honestly,' she promised, half-tempted to touch his hand to reinforce her words but not quite brave enough to do it. Even in something as small and unimportant as this she needed to maintain some degree of distance. 'You get yourself to the hospital and see what you can do to help Justina and Maddelena. Your son and I are going to have some fun.'

She swung her door open and stepped out into the

crowded oven that was San Vittorio in the middle of the morning.

'Ready, *girino*?' She opened his door and held out her hand. 'Let's go!'

'See you later, *Papà*,' he called with a nonchalant wave over his shoulder.

'Give our love to Justina and Maddelena,' Lissa reminded him as she bent for a final word before she closed the door.

'Yeah, and give them a hug from me,' Taddeo added.

The idea of Matt giving any woman a hug sent a sharp pang through her that felt suspiciously like jealousy, and Lissa was still wondering about it as they entered the toy shop. The vast display of cartoon characters that confronted her just inside the door went a long way to banishing the thoughts, at least for the foreseeable future.

It was nearly two hours later when Lissa caught sight of Matt's familiar figure out of the corner of her eye. The distraction was enough to give Taddeo a vital advantage and he struck mercilessly.

'I won!' he crowed smugly. 'I got the last piece of the treasure first. I'm the king!'

'Still having fun?' Matt queried with a grin. 'It can't do much for the ego to be beaten by a five-year-old.'

'Especially when it's the third time,' she groaned. 'I can see what they say about children picking this stuff up quicker than adults. He's an absolute whiz at it already and we've only been here for...' She glanced at her watch and did a double take. 'Goodness! I didn't realise we'd been here so long.'

'I'm sorry. I didn't think I'd be imposing on you to this extent.' He gestured towards his son who, after one brief triumphant grin at Matt, had immediately turned back to the computer screen.

'It's no imposition. I've had a wonderful time, but… I hope there wasn't a problem at the hospital?'

'Not a problem as such, but I was delayed while transportation was organised to transfer Justina and Maddelena to Altavetta.'

'Transfer them? Why? Was it something more complicated than a break after all?' Lissa would hate that to happen to her new friend. Justina was a lovely warm-hearted woman.

'Just a complicated break that's going to mean surgery for pinning and plating so we've referred her to the bigger hospital.'

'Couldn't you have done it at San Vittorio?' she asked with a frown, knowing from the coach-crash victims she'd been visiting that they had a good orthopaedic surgeon on staff. It might be a relatively small provincial hospital but its staff seemed to be second to none.

'Partly it's a case of knowing our limitations,' he admitted. 'It's a pretty nasty compound fracture of a major load-bearing bone and we don't get to deal with many of those in a day. But mainly it's because Justina's husband is our orthopaedic surgeon and she and her husband didn't feel that he ought to be the one operating on her.'

'Ah! Very understandable!' For a moment Lissa had forgotten the man's speciality but now the decision made sense. Few hospitals sanctioned a surgeon operating on a relative, especially one as close as a wife.

'And that's apart from the fact that he's away at the moment. We managed to get in contact with him and he's on his way back but we can't wait for him. We don't want to risk any complications with bleeding into the tissues of her leg, or chance a fat embolism.'

'Quite.' As a doctor dealing with such situations and decisions on a daily basis Lissa understood his criteria. 'Anyway, it's never a good idea to delay too long before the damage is repaired. I suppose you waited with the two of them until they were ready to go?'

'Actually, I drove Maddelena home so she could collect a few personal things for her mother. If I know Justina it won't be long before she bounces back and then she'll hate the idea of having visitors if she's dressed in a shapeless hospital-issue nightdress without her lipstick on.'

Lissa laughed. She could just imagine Justina's chagrin at being caught looking less than neat and tidy.

'Is *zietta* Justina really going to be all right, *Papà*?' Taddeo asked, finally abandoning the brightly coloured game to join in their conversation. There was a tiny pleat between his finely drawn brows as he looked up at the two of them. 'Did you fix her leg?'

In spite of his father's earlier assurance that his honorary aunt wasn't in danger of dying, the shadow in his eyes told Lissa that he was still worried. Matt had obviously picked up on the fact, too, if the loving hand he stroked over his son's head was any indication.

Much against her better instincts she felt her heart softening at the sight, knowing it was visible evidence of the sort of man he was under the polished exterior.

'She's going to be all right, *caro*. I promise,' he said as he crouched down to the child's height and met his eyes straight on. 'I spoke to the doctor who's going to fix her leg and told him to take special care of her for us.'

Taddeo was silent for a moment while he absorbed

the information, then he smiled. It was like seeing the sun coming up over the Adriatic in the morning.

'So that means we can go for our surprise now,' he announced with glee, almost bouncing in his eagerness. 'Where have you parked the car?'

'Ah, *mio figlio*, there won't be time for that,' Matt said ruefully. 'Because of the long journey it's too late to go now. We'll have to go another time.'

'When? Tomorrow?' He wasn't giving up on his treat easily.

'Not tomorrow.' Matt looked up at Lissa with a trapped look in his eyes. 'It will have to be on my next day off, which won't be for another week or so.'

'Does that mean I've got to wait another *week* to find out about the surprise?' His expression was tragic and mulish all at once. 'That's not fair! You promised Lissa and me a surprise and now we've got to wait another *week*.'

His little voice was rising higher and higher and Lissa was certain she could see the glitter of tears in his eyes.

Quickly, she scoured her brain for some way of averting a major scene.

'Well, *girino*, if your *papà* has disappointed us about our surprise, I think he ought to make it up to us by taking us somewhere special to eat tonight. What do you think?'

His expression went from stubborn to scheming in the blink of an eye.

'He has to take both of us?' he demanded, plainly wanting to get the rules clear. 'And it has to be tonight?'

'What do you think, *Papà*?' She glanced at Matt's bemused face. 'Are those rules fair?'

Matt made a show of heaving a very put-upon sigh

and nodded. 'That sounds fair to me. I have to take the two of you out for a meal tonight. Is that a deal?'

He held his hand out to Taddeo and Lissa had to hide a smile as the little brown paw completely disappeared inside his father's grasp while they shook on it.

'Now it's your turn,' the youngster prompted, grabbing Lissa's arm and pushing her towards his father.

'Oh, that's not necessary…' she began, but it was too late. It was her turn to feel her much smaller hand engulfed by the warm strength of Matt's.

She was in trouble, she thought as she gazed up into those dark brown eyes. Their physical contact might be limited to their two hands but the bond seemed so much greater than that. It almost felt as if…as if there was some sort of emotional connection between them.

Hormones, she dismissed shakily, retrieving her hand in a hurry and trying to decide where to hide it. If she hadn't looked at it she would have sworn that it was surrounded by some sort of electric glow as a result of the contact with his.

'So…' She had to stop to clear her throat. That husky voice certainly wasn't her normal tone. 'Where are we going to go this evening?' she managed on her second attempt.

'It's your decision,' Matt said, gesturing between the two of them. 'You have to decide my fate.'

She might have been able to break the contact between their hands but she couldn't seem to look away from that knowing gaze.

'You have to decide my fate,' he'd said, but the expression in those dark brown eyes held a challenge that made her pulse race. It certainly wasn't the result of thinking about taking his son out for a meal.

'Can we go to that restaurant in that big hotel?'

Taddeo piped up after some thought, apparently oblivious to the silent communication going on between the adults standing either side of him. 'You know, *Papà*, the one with all the nets and shells on the walls.'

Matt tried to subdue a snort of laughter as he shook his head.

'I'm afraid that one isn't open at the moment,' he said apologetically and flicked a significant glance at Lissa. 'The kitchen is having some building work done.'

'Is that the one…?' She didn't have to finish the question before he was nodding, confirming that it was the establishment that had sent the hospital so many customers over the last couple of weeks. She hadn't realised that it had already been closed down. The health and safety authorities must have been very swift off the mark in identifying the problem so fast.

'Well, then, can we buy lots of stuff and have a picnic?' His little face brightened. 'We could have it on the beach and then build a castle afterwards. Lissa's ever so good at building castles.'

'It would probably be too late for a picnic, *caro*. Remember, the sun goes down soon after seven. By the time we finished eating you would have to build your castle in the dark,' his father warned. 'That sort of thing is better in the middle of the day.'

'Well, where *can* we go?' the youngster demanded crossly, obviously not liking to be thwarted.

'You could come to my hotel,' Lissa suggested. 'It's a bit touristy, but they cook some lovely meals there.'

'Or you could come to our house and I could cook for you,' Matt offered, much to her surprise, and her breath stalled in her throat.

When had any man ever offered to cook for her? She

didn't think it had happened before in all her twenty-eight years.

'Yeah! And I could help you, *Papà*!' exclaimed Taddeo enthusiastically. 'And after we finished we could play games on the computer.'

Lissa had a strange feeling that things were whirling out of her control. Events, her emotions...

'What games? What computer?' she demanded, forcing herself to concentrate on the only thing that might make sense.

'Oh, didn't he tell you about the computer he plays on at home?' Matt enquired with an innocent lift of one dark eyebrow.

'No. He didn't,' Lissa returned sweetly, suddenly remembering just how widely Matt had grinned when his son had beaten her so soundly. 'And I suppose he's got most of the games they sell in here.'

'Most of them,' Taddeo confirmed cheekily. 'Maddelena taught me how to use the computer when she stays with me while *Papà* is at work, and *Papà* sometimes plays them with me if he comes home before my bedtime.'

Lissa hoped her glare promised retribution as Matt unrepentantly led the way out of the shop. His cheerful wave to the sales staff was enough to confirm her realisation that he was a regular customer there.

Matt's directions had been easy to follow, especially as he lived within a couple of miles of her own hotel, so Lissa should have arrived at his house calm and ready for a pleasant evening.

Unfortunately, nervous anticipation was making her tremble so much as she switched off the engine of her hired car that she might as well have just fought her way through hours of heavy city traffic.

She barely had time to look around her or draw a deep breath to subdue the butterflies when the front door was flung open.

'She's here, *Papà*! She's here!' Taddeo squealed as he scampered down the steps towards her, taking them two at a time.

'And hello to you, too.' Lissa laughed, hurrying to get out of the car in time to catch him up and whirl him around. 'Have you been waiting for me?'

'For hours and hours!' he declared. 'Come to the kitchen and see what *Papà*'s making. Are you hungry? I'm starving. Do you like bread with garlic?'

All the way down the hallway he kept up a blizzard of questions and comments without ever pausing long enough to let her speak. She barely glanced at the un-expectedly stark decoration of the villa-style house. All she could think about was the fact that she was actually here, in Matt's home, about to join him in his kitchen where he was cooking a meal for her.

'Oh, my word!' she breathed when she caught sight of the teetering mountains of dishes and saucepans piled around the work surfaces. She'd heard about men who couldn't cook a meal without using every utensil in the kitchen but until this moment she'd always thought it was an exaggeration.

The mixture of aromas swirling around her was out of this world but even they paled into insignificance when she saw the way his shorts showed off his envi-ably slim hips and long muscled legs.

'Welcome to our kitchen. I hope you're hungry,' Matt said as he turned to face her. She quickly dragged her eyes up from their lascivious perusal of his nether regions to see that he had a steaming spoon poised in mid-air with a small amount of something deep red on the tip of it.

'Careful!' she warned, but it was too late. A large drip was already on its way down the front of the heavily splattered apron he'd looped around his neck.

'Ah, well, I didn't really need to taste it again. It's already perfect,' he said with a dismissive shrug, then threw her a wicked grin as he reached for the ties at the back of the apron. 'Are you ready to begin?'

He ushered her across to the festive-looking table set in a window-lined alcove at one end of the kitchen and pulled out a chair for her.

'There is no view here at this time of night except for the lights farther down the hillside. But at breakfast, with the early morning sun pouring in through the windows...'

The expression in his eyes made her long to be here with him to share those early morning hours, especially if she'd already spend a long passionate night with him.

'I set the table, Lissa,' piped up an eager little voice to drag her out of daydreams that could never come true. 'And I put the knives and forks on the proper side, too.'

Conversation and laughter filled the next hour but she never did find out what all the dishes were called. It didn't matter because every one of them was superb— as good as, if not better than, any she'd had since she'd arrived in Italy.

'Are you sure you wouldn't like some real Italian ice cream to end the meal? Or how about some coffee?' Matt tempted but she shook her head.

'I couldn't eat another single bite.' She leant back in

her chair and groaned. 'I won't be able to move for hours, at least not without a crane.'

'*Papà* is very good at cooking, isn't he?' Taddeo declared proudly, evidence lingering at the corner of his mouth that he'd cleared his plate several times.

'Very good,' Lissa agreed wholeheartedly. 'In fact, I don't understand why the two of you aren't as big as whales if you eat like that every day.'

'Not every day,' Matt demurred. 'This was a special occasion. I don't often have so much time to spend in the kitchen, but in this instance it was imperative that I made amends for spoiling Taddeo's surprise.'

'And he has promised that we shall go and find out what it is on his next day off,' Taddeo added. 'We will tell you when it will be so you can be ready early in the morning.'

He had included her in their family outing without a second thought but, uncertain that Matt still wanted it that way, she glanced at him for confirmation.

'I'll let you know which day so you can plan accordingly,' he confirmed quietly, the expression in his eyes making her wonder if he could read her mind.

'You're sure that you want me to...'

'The surprise wouldn't be the same if she didn't come with us, would it, *caro*?'

Taddeo obviously deemed the matter settled because all he was interested in was dragging her up out of her chair to start the second part of their evening.

'Come to the computer, Lissa,' he begged. 'I've got my best game all ready to play and I'm going to beat you again.'

'I'm sure you will, *girino*, but I can't just get up from the table and leave your *papà* with all this washing-up to do. It's not fair when he did all the cooking.'

'Go on.' Matt waved her away when she went to gather up their utensils, almost as if he were shooing chickens. 'My cleaner and I have an agreement about evenings like this. I always make a terrible mess when I cook, so I have to do the cleaning, too. Tomorrow she'll come along after me and tidy things properly.'

'Come on, Lissa,' Taddeo repeated impatiently.

'Are you sure? It still doesn't seem right to eat such a wonderful meal and then walk away.'

'You can join me for a civilised cup of coffee when that monster has gone to bed,' Matt bargained. 'You'll probably need it after my son the computer shark has finished with you.'

Lissa laughed as she turned to follow Taddeo out of the room. 'At least this time I'll know I'm not being beaten by a complete novice. It takes the sting out of it a bit.'

The computer was in a room that could only be Matt's office if the number of reference books, papers and journals was anything to go by. The desk had been cleared and two chairs set ready in front of the computer and in no time she was being instructed in the finer points of her young tutor's favourite game.

In the background she was conscious of the inter-mittent clatter that told her·that the cleaning up was still in progress but it was nearly an hour later that she heard the sound of footsteps coming along the corridor to-wards them.

'All finished?' she asked brightly, turning easily in the swivel chair to watch Matt come into the room.

'Actually, I've had a bit of an accident,' he admitted, one hand holding the cloth wound tightly around the other. 'I hadn't realised I'd knocked a knife into the water until I caught my hand on it.'

Lissa was already up and out of her chair before he'd finished speaking.

'How bad is it?' she demanded as she reached for his hand. 'What damage have you done? Do you want me to drive you to San Vittorio's hospital?'

'*Papà?* Are you hurt bad?' Taddeo looked horrified and more than a little scared.

'No, *caro*. It's not so bad. I won't need to go to the hospital. I just need Lissa to help me because it's my right hand I've cut and I'm not so good at doing fiddly things like bandages with my left.'

'I presume you've got a first aid kit around somewhere?' Lissa prompted then grinned at his son in an attempt to allay his fears. 'With all the bumps and scrapes that *girino* gets into you probably need it.'

'I would need to keep a whole hospital in my kit to look after him,' Matt teased, catching on quickly to what she was trying to do.

'Well, it's not *me* this time. It's *Papà* that needs fixing,' his son pointed out smugly. 'Will you need an X-ray?'

'Nothing more than a clean-up and some sticky plaster,' Matt said dismissively. 'And by the time Lissa has finished doing it, it'll be your bedtime, so off you go.'

'But, *Papà*…!' he groaned with a longing gaze at the game still displayed on the computer screen. 'We hadn't finished our quest.'

'I'm sorry to interrupt, *caro*, but…' He shrugged and gestured towards the ungainly parcel he'd made of his hand. 'I didn't do it on purpose and I do need Lissa to help me.'

'Perhaps, if it's all right with your *papà*, I could come over another time to see if I can beat you at last?' Lissa ventured.

'Tomorrow?' he bargained hopefully. 'Straight after breakfast?'

'Lissa and I will talk about it while you're getting ready for bed,' Matt said firmly. 'Don't make a mess in the bathroom.'

'OK, *Papà*,' Taddeo agreed glumly, turning away. He'd only taken a couple of steps when he turned back. 'Lissa?' He paused a moment, glancing at his father before he continued in a rush. 'Will you come and say goodnight before I go to sleep?'

Lissa's gaze flew immediately to Matt, wondering what on earth he must be thinking about his son's unexpected request.

'If it's all right with your *papà*,' she temporised. 'And that's another thing we'll be talking about while I put his sticking plaster on.'

Taddeo heaved the sort of mammoth sigh that five-year-old boys seemed to specialise in and plodded dutifully out into the hall.

'Is he safe to have a shower by himself? Should I go and check the temperature of the water?' Lissa offered, her eyes watching the child's resigned progress towards the rituals of the end of another day.

'He's safe,' Matt said briefly, almost abruptly. 'I had an electronic gadget fitted to the shower. It governs the temperature to a pre-set level.'

At the unexpected sharpness in his tone Lissa turned to gaze at him, wondering if she'd angered him with her questions. One look at his face told her that his clipped speech had another cause entirely.

'Sit down, Matt, before you fall down,' she ordered quickly, spinning the chair Taddeo had just vacated round to position it just behind his knees.

'I'm all right,' he insisted, shaking his head and blinking.

'You wouldn't say that if you could see your face. It's grey and clammy with sweat,' she said bluntly and grabbed his elbow to tug him back towards the chair. 'Now, sit!'

'Yes, Doctor!' he said but it came out too weakly to sound like the joke he'd intended.

'Exactly how much damage *have* you done?' Lissa demanded as she reached for the edge of the towel, and had to stifle a gasp when she flipped back the top layer and saw how darkly stained the rest of the cloth had become. 'So much blood! Have you cut your wrist?'

'Nothing so bad as that. Mostly it's a minor flesh wound but I've just nicked a vein in the thenar eminence.'

Lissa didn't need to unwrap the final layer covering the fleshy mound at the base of his thumb to know that the bleeding hadn't stopped. 'Your veins are still distended from having your hands in the hot water. The bleeding isn't going to slow down until we can get some ice on it.'

She paused to look him over carefully. His colour was a little better but the wound was obviously painful. At least he didn't look as if he was going to keel over now.

'Where do you keep your first-aid kit and how extensive is it?'

'It's in the bathroom and it's a pretty extensive one,' he said as he prepared to stand.

'Hang on a minute.' She put her hand on his shoulder to keep him still. 'Taddeo's in the bathroom and we don't want to do this in front of him. All that blood will frighten him.'

'No problem. My medical supplies are in *my* bathroom, safely locked away from prying hands,' he explained laboriously, his eyes closed tightly. 'And I would be very glad if we could get there some time soon because this is rather painful.'

Silently she looped her arm around him and urged him to his feet then tightened her grip as he swayed momentarily.

'I'm all right,' Matt muttered as he set off slowly, but she didn't know whether his words were for himself or for her.

It probably didn't take more than a minute or two to cover the distance to his *en suite* bathroom but it seemed a great deal longer while she worried about what she'd do if he started to fall. He was so much bigger and heavier than she was that they'd probably both hit the floor, and as for getting him up again...

'It's in there,' he said gruffly, gesturing towards the cupboard under the large plain white basin then groaning as he went to lower himself to perch on the side of the bath and jarred his hand. 'There's a childproof lock,' he finished through gritted teeth.

Lissa negotiated the lock the first time and opened the doors to reach for the state-of-the-art container inside.

There was another childproof lock to deal with on the container itself and then she had it open on the wide marble surround beside the basin.

'OK, now let's see what you've done to yourself,' she invited, drawing a deep breath as she turned to begin her task.

Matt drew air in through his teeth in a sharp hiss when she began to take the last layer off and she paused, fearful that it was her fault.

One part of her brain was functioning perfectly normally, continuously monitoring his breathing and the colour of his skin as she carefully unwrapped his injury. The other part was cringing at the very thought that she might be causing him pain and fear that she might not be able to give him the help he needed.

'Oh, Matt!' she whispered, aghast when she finally saw the extent of the injury. 'Are you sure you don't want me to take you to the hospital? You might need a neurologist to have a look at this, or a plastic surgeon at least.'

'That's not an option as we don't have either on full-time staff. At this time of day it would mean travelling all the way to Altavetta and, anyway, it's not necessary.'

'How do you know it's not necessary?' she demanded heatedly, only just remembering in time to keep her voice down. It wouldn't do the situation any good if Taddeo came running in to see what they were shouting about.

'Think about it,' she pleaded. 'If you've damaged the nerve supply you could end up with a useless thumb. Then what good will you be as an emergency physician?'

'I haven't damaged the nerve supply, so don't worry about that. It's just the bleeding...'

'How do you *know* you haven't?' she persisted. She was suddenly aware that her concern for him was so much greater than for any other patient because, in spite of her determination to the contrary, she'd become emotionally involved with him. The thought that he might be permanently maimed if she didn't make the right decision, or didn't persuade him to follow the right course of action...

'I know I haven't cut any nerves because I tested my neurological reflexes,' he said calmly and logically.

'You tested…? When?' she demanded. 'When did you test them? How?'

'Before I wrapped my hand up and came to find you,' he said with a forced show of patience. 'I used the point of the same knife that did the damage to check that I still had full sensation and movement right to the tip of the thumb. Once I knew that I didn't need any specialist treatment, I knew you were the best person to put me back together.'

He gave her the same endearing grin his son had perfected before he continued. 'Don't forget, I've seen how good your embroidery is, and it's a lot better than young Paolo's.'

'Is that who's on duty tonight?' she asked stiffly as she began to locate the supplies she'd need. She was trying not to picture him standing over the sink with his hand dripping blood while he used the tip of a blood-stained knife as a substitute pin to check his neurological reflexes.

'The one and only. Oh, don't get me wrong,' he added quickly. 'In a while he's going to be a very good emergency physician, but just at the moment and for this particular injury, I'd rather be in the hands of some-one who's fully trained and very good at what she does.'

'Either that's a genuine compliment or you're trying to butter me up so I'll do my best,' she teased, prefer-ring to keep up a conversation than to have to work in silence while he supervised what she was doing. It might also help to control the fine tremor in her hands at the thought of having to perform even a minor pro-cedure on him. This wasn't going to be a quick two-minute job and the way her hormones reacted each time she was anywhere near him…

'It's a genuine compliment, Lissa, but it's also supposed to persuade you to hurry up and get some analgesic into the damned thing to stop it hurting.'

'Right.' She switched deliberately into professional mode. 'You know what you've got in here better than I do. Which analgesic have you got and what sort of sutures do you want?'

CHAPTER EIGHT

'HAVE you got any sterile water or shall I use tap water?' Lissa asked as she repositioned the cork-topped stool more conveniently beside the basin where the light positioned over Matt's shaving mirror would provide the level of illumination she needed.

She gestured for him to sit on it then hovered protectively behind him as he made the move, still not convinced that he wasn't going to fall.

'I keep a sealed pouch of sterile water in the fridge, but my hand is already clean enough. There are ampoules of lignocaine and needles—'

'Your hand is *not* clean enough,' she contradicted swiftly. 'You've had it soaking in water full of microscopic food particles. No matter how neatly I put you back together, if you've got a contaminated wound...'

'All right. All right. Do what you think best,' he conceded. 'All I can say is that I feel like a wimp when you think that John Wayne could fight to a standstill with his body full of bullets.'

'His wounds were just clever make-up,' she pointed out, still smiling as she hurried back to the kitchen.

It was strange to see this vulnerable side to such a strong man. Was it the first time he'd had to face an injury? She would hardly have thought so if his son's adventurousness was anything to go by.

'Hold your hand over the sink,' she directed when she returned with the chilled sterile water. 'Apart from cleaning the wound this should also constrict the blood vessels to slow down the bleeding.'

Matt stoically endured as she irrigated the wound thoroughly and she was amused to see that he closed his eyes when she injected the analgesic around the margins of it.

He didn't relax until she tested his sensitivity a couple of minutes later by pressing the skin with a gloved finger.

'Can't feel a thing, thank God,' he muttered then leant forwards for a closer look. 'How many sutures do you think it's going to take?'

'As many as it takes,' she said sweetly as she stepped between him and his hand, effectively blocking his view. 'Just relax and I'll get it over as quickly as I can.'

He muttered under his breath and asked several times how the job was going, but by the time she straightened up to reach for a dressing to cover the area she was well pleased with her efforts.

'Am I allowed to see what you've done before you hide it away?' he requested politely, but a glance at his face told her that if she didn't agree, he'd soon have the dressing off once she was out of the door.

'There you are,' she said as she stepped aside to reveal a neat line of sutures. 'It shouldn't cause too much of a problem if you want a fortune-teller to read your palm.'

He turned his hand to the light and peered closely at it before looking up at her.

'I knew you'd do an excellent job,' he said with quiet satisfaction. 'And I *am* grateful although it might not have sounded like it to begin with.' He stared down at the wound again for a long moment before he continued softly. 'Since... Since Taddeo was born, I find it…difficult…no, almost impossible to cope with situations when they're not under my control. I don't like to have to rely on other people to do things for me.'

She remembered how uncomfortable he'd been about asking her to keep an eye on Taddeo while he went in to the hospital to check up on Justina.

'But Maddelena takes care of Taddeo all the time,' she pointed out with a frown. 'Isn't that a contradiction?'

'I pay her for her time,' he said simply and suddenly she understood his reasoning. He might need someone to look after his son, but because he paid her to do it he still maintained overall control of the situation.

'*Papà!* I'm ready!' Taddeo called. 'Has Lissa fixed your finger?'

'I've nearly finished,' Lissa called back.

'Be with you in a minute,' Matt added as she reached for a dressing to cover her handiwork. 'Choose the book you want to read, *caro*, and climb into bed.'

She worked in silence for a moment, her thoughts more on enjoying this brief insight into their nightly routine than performing a task she'd done a thousand times.

He tried to object when she began to support his hand in a sling but she fixed him with a stern look.

'You know as well as I do that you need to keep this elevated,' she lectured. 'You can wiggle your fingers at intervals to keep the circulation going, but otherwise that hand is officially out of commission until the stitches come out.'

He pulled a face, but must have realised that she wasn't to be swayed, especially when she was right.

'All right, then. Truss me up like a turkey if you must,' he said in a resigned tone and turned so that she could reach to position the large triangle of synthetic fabric. 'Just as long as you remember to give me my kiss to make it better.'

In her surprise Lissa fumbled the knot at the back of his neck and had to start again.

'Kiss?' It came out more like a squeak than a real word.

'Of course,' he said, apparently totally serious if his expression was to be believed. 'It won't get better if I don't get my kiss. You ask Taddeo.'

Lissa couldn't speak. Her heart was suddenly beating at twice its normal rate while her breathing had stopped altogether. Could he possibly be saying what it sounded like?

She sneaked another glance at his face but without being able to see his eyes clearly she had no idea if he was just teasing.

Playing for time, she checked to make sure she hadn't made the sling too short, then leant forwards to press her lips gently to the thickly protective padding over his bandaged thumb.

'That won't work,' he protested plaintively. 'There's too many dressings in the way. Here...' Taking her by surprise, he turned to face her and pulled her into the open angle between his knees. 'This is much better.'

As she watched in a mixture of horror, amazement and fascination he ostentatiously closed his eyes as he tilted his head back and pursed his lips.

Just one look at that mouth waiting for hers was enough to take the starch out of her knees but she didn't have the courage to take him up on the invitation.

'Well?' he prompted, opening one eye to find her frozen in indecision. 'I'm waiting.'

'But, I… You… It's your hand, not…' she faltered almost incoherently.

'Oh, for goodness' sake,' he said impatiently and straightened up off the stool. 'Don't you know that kisses travel?'

Before she knew what was happening he'd wrapped his free arm around her shoulders and pulled her against him, his head already dipping so that their lips could meet.

Time and space ceased to exist as she experienced the sweetest, tenderest, sexiest kiss of her entire life.

It was everything she'd been trying not to imagine ever since she'd first met him two weeks ago, only better.

He held her with an enticing mixture of gentleness and strength that invited her to trust while his mouth was soft and warm and infinitely inviting, tempting her to respond in a wholehearted way she would never have imagined possible.

This was not the wet onslaught of a novice, or the rough aggression of a man more interested in his own pleasure.

Never before had she realised that having a man's tongue breach her lips to explore the secrets beyond could send a sharp spiral of arousal right to the depths of her body. Never before had she wanted to open her mouth and tempt him into a duel; never before had she wanted to merge her body with his so that they became one in every sense of the word.

'*Papà?* Are you coming?' demanded a little voice, piercing the cocoon of their self-absorbed isolation.

Matt groaned and muttered something under his breath as he cradled her head against his shoulder for a few timeless seconds.

'I'm coming,' he called back in a noticeably breathless voice that salved Lissa's embarrassment. She was so stunned by her response to him that she hardly knew where she was. At least he seemed to have been equally as affected.

'I'll just tidy these things away,' she offered, needing a moment to herself before she had to face Taddeo's eagle eyes. 'What do you want me to do with the sharps?'

She tried to step away from him but he tightened his arm around her.

'Lissa. Look at me,' he whispered. 'Please.'

Hesitantly she raised her gaze from the open first-aid kit to eyes that seemed even darker brown than usual. The light over the basin was almost bright enough to be a spotlight but she could see that he'd regained most of his colour now that he was out of pain.

'I didn't intend for that to happen,' he said softly and her heart sank. She'd just experienced the most wonderful kiss of her life and he was going to spoil it.

'It was intended as a joke…a tease? I don't know.' He broke off to stare up at the ceiling, running his fingers through his hair and leaving it in spiky disarray before he suddenly focused on her again.

'I'll apologise, if you want me to, but I won't lie,' he declared fiercely. 'I won't tell you I regret it because I don't. I've been wanting to kiss you for weeks.'

Lissa was left standing there with her mouth open as he strode out of the bathroom on his way to Taddeo's room.

It shouldn't have taken her more than two minutes to dispose of the debris from such a minor operation but her brain was so scrambled that she couldn't seem to force her hands to work properly.

It was nearly ten minutes before she followed the enticing sound of Matt's voice and found herself in the doorway to Taddeo's room.

They were so busy with their story that they hadn't noticed her arrive so she stayed where she was, watching.

This was the one room in the house that was full of colour and life, from the posters on the walls to the brightly painted furniture and plastic box overflowing with toys. But there was only one thing that drew her eyes like a magnet—the two dark heads bent over the book spread out on Taddeo's pyjama'd knees, his little body cradled against the much larger one of his father by his unrestricted arm.

It was a picture right out of her dearest longings and her heart melted inside her.

How many times had she imagined just such a picture, with her child cradled on his father's knee while he told the story chosen for that night? How many times had she pictured the way he would giggle, just as Taddeo was giggling, when his father put on silly voices for each of the characters in the story? Just looking at the two of them together like this made her feel warm and happy inside.

Unfortunately, there were two things wrong with the picture…Matt wasn't her husband and Taddeo wasn't her child.

She must have made a sound because suddenly both of them were looking at her. The expression of pleasure in their dark eyes was subtly different but there were almost identical smiles of welcome on their faces.

'Lissa! You're late! *Papà* has already started the story,' Taddeo exclaimed. 'Come and sit next to me so you can see the pictures.'

When she hesitated Matt seconded the invitation but the expression in his eyes wasn't nearly so candid.

'Yes, Lissa. Come and sit next to us so you can find out if the sky is really falling down.'

There was a sweet pain in leaning close to the two of them to share the book, knowing that it was a once-in-a-lifetime thing. One half of her mind was relishing every nuance, from the fresh soapy smell of Taddeo's skin to the deep resonance of Matt's voice. The other half was desperately trying to preserve even a little distance so that when she was no longer part of their circle, her heart wouldn't forever mourn their loss.

All too soon the story was over and in spite of pleas for 'just one more' Matt stood firm.

'Say goodnight to Lissa,' he instructed as he straightened the lightweight bedclothes that were all the child would need on such a warm night.

'Goodnight, Lissa,' Taddeo said obediently. 'And thank you for fixing my *papà*'s hand.'

As though he had just remembered something important, he sat up in bed again.

'*Papà*, did she remember to kiss it better?' he demanded, clearly concerned.

'Yes, *caro*, she did,' he said with a secret wink for Lissa that brought sudden warmth to her cheeks.

'Did she kiss the *bleeding* bit?' he asked with a horrified grimace.

'No, no. That wasn't necessary. Don't you remember? Kisses can travel.'

'Did it work?' he demanded, his gaze showing just how fascinated he was by the injury hidden in such an impressive way.

'Of course it worked. I can't feel a thing,' he confirmed with another quick glance in Lissa's direction.

'Now, shut your eyes or you'll still be awake when tomorrow comes and you'll be too tired to play.' He bent to press a tender kiss of his own to the smooth forehead and stroked a loving hand over tousled dark hair. 'Sleep well, *caro*.'

He led the way out of the room, pausing only to turn off the light and pull the door almost closed.

'Now, how about that coffee, or would you prefer something stronger?' he offered as he made for the kitchen.

The phone started ringing before she'd even answered.

'*Pronto!*' he said into the receiver, shaking his head when she would have backed out of the room to give him privacy for his call.

It could have been almost anyone phoning him at this time of an evening. She'd even seen quite young children out with their families until long after ten o'clock at night so it wouldn't necessarily be someone from the hospital with an emergency.

Perhaps it was a woman...

'Maddelena! I'm glad you phoned. How is your mother?' Matt demanded, and Lissa realised with a swift burst of something that felt suspiciously like relief that her presence wouldn't be an intrusion after all. Although why she should be feeling relieved was another matter entirely, and one she wasn't going to think about until she was at least a couple of miles away from the man on the other side of the room.

She couldn't help herself from watching him as he strode backwards and forwards and had to smother a smile when she saw how hampered he was by his restricted arm. She'd noticed before that he tended to 'speak' with his hands and now, with one holding the phone and the other out of commission, it was almost as if he couldn't speak properly.

Finally he ended the call and she had to abandon her amusement at his expense.

'Justina is doing well?' she asked, although she'd been able to gather that much from his satisfied expression.

'Very well. The operation was a complete success. She should be able to transfer back to San Vittorio in a couple of days to be closer to her family and friends.'

While he was speaking he'd been trying to fill and assemble a traditional espresso coffee-maker. He'd reached the stage of screwing the two halves together and in spite of the fact that he must have realised he wasn't going to have enough hands free he wouldn't give in.

Before Lissa could reach him, the inevitable happened.

'*Dio!*' he exclaimed as coffee-grounds and water seemed to explode around him and all down the front of his clothes, the two halves of the espresso pot landing up on the floor.

'It's a good job that's made of metal,' Lissa commented straight-faced as she bent to pick them up, then bent again with a handful of paper towel to mop up the mess.

Matt was still standing there when she straightened up. Even his sling was liberally splattered with clumps of coffee grounds.

'What a good job that it happened when the water was still cold, or this time I'd be treating you for scalds,' she commented and turned to deposit the soggy paper in the bin.

When he didn't answer she turned back and found

him looking down at the front of his trousers, and she realised they'd been completely soaked in a broad swathe right across the front.

Slowly his eyes lifted to hers and held.

This time she wasn't in any doubt about his thoughts, especially as she'd just spoken about treating him. She knew without either of them having to say a word that he was thinking about the little childish ritual of 'kissing it better'.

Her eyes flicked down and then up again with almost guilty speed and when she saw the new heat in his eyes she knew that he had the same X-rated image in his mind.

'*Dio!* Don't do this to me, woman,' he groaned and closed his eyes. 'I can't even go and have a cold shower.'

'I thought you'd just had one,' she retorted with a helpless chuckle, marvelling at the new courage that was suddenly flowing through her veins. She'd never been adept at the sort of male-female banter that her colleagues seemed so good at, but somehow, just knowing that there was something about her that had an effect on Matt...

He tried to glare at her but couldn't maintain it in the face of her mirth.

'Do you need some help getting out of those clothes?' she offered when their laughter had died away, then realised what she'd said and was off again.

'What are you trying to do to me?' he complained with a theatrical scowl. 'How am I supposed to remember that my son is asleep just a few metres away when you're offering to take my clothes off?'

She was fighting a grin again, but to little avail, finally giving in to a quiet chuckle when he stomped off in the direction of his bedroom with a muttered, 'I'll manage, thank you.'

He would probably never know just how much good he'd done her ego over the last hour or so, she thought as she put a fresh measure of coffee in the espresso-maker and filled the reservoir to the line with water. With two good hands it was a simple matter to screw the two halves together and place it on the hotplate.

'Do you want milk in yours?' she offered when he reappeared some ten minutes later wearing a tracksuit with an elastic waist. She'd been wondering how he was going to manage to fasten the waistband on an ordinary pair of trousers.

'Please.' He was preoccupied with trying to sort out the sling, having had to remove it to replace his wet shirt.

She brought the cup over and set it down on the table. 'Here. Let me,' she offered, touching him on his shoulder to turn him round.

'Lissa…' There was a warning tone in his voice that make her withdraw instantly, her hand left hovering in mid-air.

'What?' she whispered, suddenly nervous enough that she felt like taking several large steps backwards. There was an electric charge in the air around them that she'd never felt before. She could almost hear it crackle.

He closed his eyes and drew in a deep breath as if he was having to fight for control.

She was close enough to be able to count every eye-lash as they lay in fans on his slightly flushed cheeks and to see the dark shadow of his newly emerged beard.

His hair was ruffled again, probably as a result of pulling on his tracksuit top, and her fingers itched to smooth it into position, wondering if the stray glints of sun-bleached gold that the artificial light struck among the dark strands would make it feel warm to the touch.

The silence went on for several long minutes before he broke it, minutes in which she helplessly let her eyes roam over features that were rapidly becoming as familiar to her as her own.

'I'm sorry…' he said suddenly, his voice husky and strained. 'The analgesic is starting to wear off and I need to ask…'

His voice died away when their eyes met, the messages that flashed between them needing no words.

She didn't know whether she moved towards him first or he reached for her but in an instant she was in his arms and their mouths were fused in blatant hunger.

Long moments later, when she was almost at the point of spontaneous combustion, he suddenly wrenched his mouth away from hers and shook his head.

'Ah, Lissa, no,' he said breathlessly, resting his forehead against hers almost as if even that distance between them was too far. 'This is neither the time nor the place. We must talk. I need to ask you… Lissa, will you stay here with me?'

'Stay?' she whispered, amazed at the suddenness of the request, at the bluntness of it. There was no subtlety or tenderness and certainly no promises, and she was conscious of a crushing feeling of…of disappointment. It seemed so unlike the Matt she thought she was getting to know.

'You know I don't like to ask favours,' he continued, his words startling her out of her thoughts. 'But in spite of my injury I have to go to the hospital tomorrow— just to supervise, I promise—and Maddelena is staying overnight with friends in Altavetta to be close to her mother. She's staying there until Justina's transferred back to San Vittorio and that means there would be no one here with Taddeo when he wakes up in the morning.'

Anticlimax was too tame a word for the way she felt.

She'd actually thought he was propositioning her when all he wanted was for her to babysit his son for a few hours.

What an idiot she was!

Thank goodness he couldn't read her mind or he'd be laughing himself silly, she thought dismally. What a fool she was to have thought it for even a moment! He knew that she was returning to England in just a couple of weeks. Why on earth would he court heartache by embarking on a liaison that had so little time to run its course?

'So, will you stay?' he prompted. 'I know you haven't got any clothes with you but I've got a spare toothbrush and I could lend you a shirt or something to sleep in.'

While he'd been speaking he'd gradually eased away from her until now he was only holding her hand.

She glanced down at it and couldn't help noticing how much larger and darker his was, his fingers long and lean with the well-tended nails of someone who was very aware of hygiene. They looked like a surgeon's hands, deft and controlled. What would they be like as a lover's?

No point thinking about that, she reminded herself sternly. It wasn't even a possibility. At least she could give Matt points for not leading her on. The mistaken idea had all been on her side.

'Of course, I'll stay,' she said with a silent sigh.

Was there ever any doubt that she would agree? He

must have known that she wouldn't have been able to sleep if she knew that he was having difficulty finding someone to stay with Taddeo. Especially when she had nothing better to do. 'I can wash out my things and they'll be ready by the morning. All you need to do is wake me when you leave.'

Matt stood beside the bed with his uninjured hand curled into a tight fist. It was either that, or he would be reaching out to touch her.

Had there ever been a more beautiful woman than Lissa?

She didn't release her hair often, preferring to tie the dark shoulder-length curls out of the way during the day. But that didn't mean that he hadn't imagined her like this, the archetypal fairy-tale princess with that dark profusion spread over the pristine white of the pillow.

Of course, when he'd imagined it, her curls had been a riot across *his* pillow, with his face buried in them to draw in the honeyed tang of the perfume she wore.

Or was it the scent of her skin? Even after kissing her he couldn't be sure, but he was only too willing to explore the possibilities.

He sighed when what he wanted to do was groan aloud.

Look at him, as pathetic as a teenager mooning over a picture of his favourite actress or pop-singer. He'd never had time for such things in his youth but he'd certainly seemed to have been making up for lost time over the last couple of weeks or so.

Had it really been such a short time since this woman had barged her way into his life? She'd actually started ordering him about in her efforts to secure the best care for the child of a stranger—his son.

Since then he'd vacillated between wanting to spend time in her company and wanting to stay as far as possible away from her. What premonition was it that had warned him that his life was never going to be the same?

He certainly wasn't the same.

For five years he had deliberately avoided any but the most superficial contact with women. Now it was some ungodly hour of the morning and here he was standing in the silence of his own guest room just so that he could be close to this beautiful, evasive, charming, alluring, *frustrating* woman.

It hadn't helped that the first thing he'd seen when he'd walked into his bathroom this morning had been those little scraps of ivory silk and lace that she'd rinsed out and hung over one of the navy towels he'd left out for her. He hadn't needed to know in such detail exactly what she wore next to her skin.

The fact that it was his T-shirt sliding off one honey-gold shoulder wasn't helping either, not when he didn't know whether he wanted to pull it up to save his sanity or pull it down so that he could see more.

Except he wouldn't just want to look.

He drew in a deep steadying breath and blew it out slowly.

OK. Let's go back to that basic psychology course, he argued silently. The admission that he couldn't stay away was galling, especially when he prided himself on being in control of every aspect of his life. The realisation that he was barely able to stop himself from touching her was sobering, too, but at least it brought some measure of calm. According to the lectures he'd attended, acknowledging the problem was half of the battle. Perhaps now he could set about finding a solution.

Whatever the solution was, it certainly didn't involve waking Lissa up early so that they could eat breakfast together. The best thing he could do for both of them was leave her to sleep until it was time for him to go.

He'd taken only a single step backwards when her eyes opened and seemed to mesh with his, almost as though she'd known he would be there.

As he stood rooted to the floor with his breath trapped in his throat, feeling utterly foolish at being caught, she smiled at him and the sweet power of it nearly brought him to his knees.

'Good morning,' she whispered, her voice early-morning husky but not showing any surprise at finding him there.

There was a long pause while he tried to find something rational to say but he was completely tongue-tied.

'Perhaps this is a dream?' she continued with a slight frown pleating her forehead, her eyes still dark and drowsy. 'Perhaps you're the prince coming to wake the Sleeping Beauty with a kiss.'

A kiss.

The word was barely more than a breath on the air but once she'd uttered it he couldn't think about anything else. Well, he'd hardly thought about anything else since their first one so that was nothing new.

She was still gazing up at him with those eyes the colour of the dark honey she was named after, and he was powerless to look away. He could feel himself being drawn closer and closer to her without having to move a millimetre.

He knew it was impossible.

He knew it was wrong, but he couldn't stop himself

from taking that last silent step that brought him back
to the side of her bed.

As if it were happening in a dream, he went down
on one knee and leant towards her, his eyes now fixed
on the soft promise of her waiting lips.

CHAPTER NINE

'WHEN you've finished your breakfast we'll go to my hotel so I can change my clothes,' Lissa told Taddeo, desperate to fill the silence that fell each time he put another spoonful into his mouth.

Even so she couldn't stop her mind replaying Matt's visit to her borrowed room.

Had she really believed it was a dream or had she just been fooling herself? Had it been a way to give herself licence to invite Matt's kisses without feeling guilty?

However it had started out, the minute his lips had touched hers it had become vividly, stunningly real, from the weight of his body pressing down on hers to the damp silk of his hair slipping through her fingers; the tantalising excitement of his hand slipping under the hem of her makeshift nightdress to explore her pliant body to the guttural moan he uttered when she arched against him.

What would have happened if the alarm function on his watch hadn't gone off, she didn't know. Would he have called a halt before he'd given in to her implied invitation or would she have come to her senses before he'd stripped off his clothes and joined her in the bed?

All she knew was that she hadn't been able to meet his eyes when he'd uttered a broken apology and left the room.

What she was finding so difficult to face was the fact that she hadn't honestly wanted him to stop.

It wasn't just that she'd recovered from the devastation of her one and only previous relationship to want to try again. It was the fact that for the first time in her life she'd actually felt as if she hadn't had a choice in the matter.

It was almost frightening to realise that in her past she'd always felt almost...detached when a man had kissed her. As if one part of her brain had been an onlooker telling her what she should be doing and feeling.

This morning there had been no observer. Every part of her, brain and body, had been willingly involved in what had been happening.

And the crazy thing was that, in her heart of hearts, she didn't care. The woman who had always wanted to wait for her wedding night to give herself to the man she loved had been willing to surrender to—

'Finished!' Taddeo announced as he clambered down from the table with his empty bowl in one hand and his spoon in the other. He trotted across and reached up to deposit them on the draining board. 'And I remembered to put them ready for the washing-up.'

'Good boy,' she praised and his delighted smile told her she'd given the right response.

It was obviously part of his daily routine and Lissa found herself wondering just how many other such little facets there were to life with Matteo and Taddeo Aldarini.

A fist tightened around her heart when she forced herself to remember that she was unlikely ever to know. No matter that his father seemed to desire her every bit as fiercely as she had grown to want him, she was just a fleeting part of their lives.

'Are we going to your hotel now? Is it the one with

the shells and the nets in the restaurant? Could we go in there for a drink?' He was hopping from one foot to the other and clearly had plenty of energy to burn.

Lissa had a momentary pang of anxiety. What on earth was she doing, taking charge of a young lively little boy like this? She was a complete novice where childcare was concerned. Every time she'd seen him before there had been another adult with them, except for their outing to the computer shop.

'Oh, good. I can sit in the front!' he crowed when they went out to her car.

'Oh, no, you can't, young man,' she contradicted. 'Your *papà* has a rule about you sitting in the back with your seat belt on.'

'But this is *your* car,' he pointed out. 'You can make your own rules.'

'But you are *his* son, so I have to obey *his* rules,' she countered, ushering him and his pout of displeasure into the back.

His bad mood barely lasted to the end of the road as he began a running commentary on everything he could see out of the window. By the time she'd escorted him up in the lift to her hotel room and had raided the mini-refrigerator for a bottle of juice he was on top form.

'Wow. Your room is bigger than *Papà*'s, and you've got two beds. Is that so you can have a friend to stay with you or do you sleep in one bed one night and then in the other?'

Lissa was keeping one ear on his chatter while she raided her wardrobe for clean clothes, knowing that he rarely left time for answers. It didn't take long to don a cool cotton top and a pair of drawstring trousers and slip her feet into espadrilles.

She was just contemplating the wisdom of taking her

wash kit and a change of clothing with her in case Matt needed her to stay over for another night when she was suddenly forced to tune into Taddeo's questions again.

'Has my *papà* slept in one of your beds, Lissa?' he asked cheerfully, shocking her speechless. 'They'd be big enough so his feet didn't hang over the end.'

'No!' she gasped when she'd caught her breath. 'He's got his own bed at your house, remember.'

'Hmm.' He nodded thoughtfully and she wondered what was going on in his head now. It wasn't long before she found out.

'Do you love my *papà*?' he demanded suddenly, looking very serious.

This time—the one time when she would have liked him to rabbit on about the next topic to leap into his busy little head without waiting for an answer—this time he just stood there with those big dark eyes fixed intently on her.

'He's a wonderful *papà* and a wonderful doctor, too,' she said with a big smile pinned on her face. Anything to disguise the shock she'd felt when her initial response had been to say yes.

'I know that. But do you *love* him?' he persisted. 'Because it won't work unless you do.'

'What won't work?' She sat down on the edge of one of the beds with her thoughts reeling. How could she possibly unravel the mysterious workings of the mind of a five-year-old when she didn't even know what was going on in her own?

Had she really fallen in love with Matteo Aldarini? How on earth could she be sure? After all, she'd hardly shown good judgement with her last foray into matters of the heart.

'I told *Papà* that I wanted you to come and live with

us, but he said that only married people could do that. So then I told him he should marry you, but he said that it would only work if the man and the woman loved each other. So I need to know if you love *Papà* so you can marry him and you can come and live with us for ever and ever.'

'Ah, *girino*, if only it was that easy,' Lissa said softly.

'That's what *Papà* said,' he declared in tones of disgust. 'But it *is* easy. I know that I love *Papà*, and I know I love you.'

Touched to the depths of her heart, Lissa held her arms out to him. 'And I love you, too,' she said in a choked voice, knowing it was true and knowing, too, that it was going to break her heart if she never saw him again after she went back to England.

He was such a bright, irrepressible, loving little boy and she would have loved to watch him grow to maturity but…some things were just not meant to be. If Matt had fallen in love with her, he wouldn't have had to let Taddeo down so gently.

'Hey! It's a beautiful day out there, *girino*,' she exclaimed, determined not to wallow. 'What are we doing shut up inside a hotel when we could be checking up on your *papà* to make sure he's not using his poorly hand, and taking him out for a picnic lunch.'

'Yeah! A picnic! Come on, Lissa. Hurry up! Let's go and get *Papà*.' Suddenly he was a five-year-old child again, wildly excited about a treat rather than seriously trying to sort out his father's love life.

Lissa hadn't been certain how she was going to face Matt after their torrid kiss that morning, but her conversation with Taddeo had solved the problem at a stroke.

Knowing that he hadn't changed his mind about starting a permanent relationship didn't affect the fact that
he obviously desired her, but until she'd managed to get
her own emotions under control, she would just have to
make sure that she didn't spend any time alone with
him.

Their picnic was a great success.

Taddeo had insisted that they go to 'their' beach with
the basket full of goodies. Once there, they had rapidly
ended up as part of a far larger group of people, most
of whom seemed to be related to Justina.

Once again, there were plenty of people to vie against
in mad games of volleyball and football, and plenty of
younger children for Taddeo to play with without getting up to too much mischief.

Best of all there were plenty of people to talk to so that
she and Matt didn't have to speak to each other at all.

Her foresight in packing a change of clothing came
in handy as Matt said he had been called in to the hospital to supervise for a sick colleague. Lissa had no way
of knowing if it was true, but she was able to persuade
herself that she was relieved that she and Taddeo were
going to have the villa to themselves for the night.

The two of them were still sitting at the breakfast
table the next morning, discussing what they were going
to do for the day, when she heard the sound of a key
in the lock.

Every nerve sprang to attention and her eyes fixed on
the kitchen door, longing to see Matt walk into view.
In spite of her resolve to put a sensible distance between
them, it seemed like days since she'd last seen him and
she'd missed him more than she dared to admit.

Except it was Maddelena who rounded the corner
with a big grin for Taddeo and wide-open arms.

'Did you miss me, monster?' she demanded, giving him a noisy kiss. 'Have you been a good boy for Lissa?'

'Of course I've been good, haven't I, Lissa?'

'Not bad,' she said grudgingly, then smiled at the two of them. 'Except for the day he went to the computer shop with me and pretended he didn't know the games, then kept beating me!'

'Ha! Well, he won't be winning any more, because I'm better than he is,' Maddelena taunted, deliberately starting a 'no, you aren't', 'yes, I am' war.

Lissa could see why Taddeo got on so well with her. She certainly seemed to know how to deal with him on his own level, but then, with her enormous extended family, she'd had far more practice than Lissa ever would.

As she collected up their used dishes and cutlery Lissa stifled a pang of sadness that she was now redundant. It wouldn't take her long to collect her few belongings and then it would be back to the solitude of her hotel room.

Anyway, it was about time she started giving some thought to what she was going to do when she returned home. There was the small matter of a job to find and a future to plan.

Lissa flopped back on her bed and stared at the ceiling, her eyes forced wide open as she tried to stop the tears falling.

Taddeo had wanted her to stay with them and Maddelena had tried to persuade her to keep them company for the morning, at least until Matt finished work, but Lissa had stood firm. There was only so long that she could put on a brave face when she could feel something perfect slipping away from her and knew that there was nothing she could do about it.

Now, at least, there was no one to see her if she cried as if her heart were breaking. If she hid away in her room there would be no one to whom she would have to admit that it was already broken.

Her face was red and blotchy by the time the tears began to ebb but her heart didn't feel any lighter.

She still had more than a week left of her holiday. She could hardly sit in her room that long, but how was she going cope if she were to bump into Matt and Taddeo? San Vittorio was only a small place, after all.

She would be devastated if the first time she saw the two of them she burst into tears.

Where was the cool calm and collected young woman who had arrived on the Adriatic coast such a short time ago? She'd been so certain that she had all her emotions under control. She'd been so determined that she wasn't going to allow anyone to get too close to her again.

Ha! So much for determination and certainty! She'd barely been here for two days when she'd started to lose her heart to Matteo Aldarini. Now she had to face the prospect that it might belong to him for the rest of her life.

'Melodramatic nonsense!' she declared aloud and sat up sharply. 'What I need is a purpose, not this lolling around feeling sorry for myself.'

She frowned as she contemplated her options and in the end decided there were just two.

'My first option is to stay on and finish my holiday— after all, it's paid for. Alternatively, I enquire about the possibility of returning to England early and starting my job hunt.'

She searched out the diary that had slipped its way

to the bottom of her handbag to find out exactly how many days were involved. It was so easy to lose track of time when there wasn't the routine of work to remind her.

She found it at last and flicked through until she came to the right page then froze.

There were several entries for this week but only one of them, today's entry, had been scored out so heavily that not a single letter was legible. It was almost impossible to remember her happiness when she'd written 'Wedding Day' on that page all those months ago.

Lissa sat and stared at the evidence waiting for the misery to descend but it didn't happen. All she felt was an echo of the anger that had consumed her when she'd scored the words out, but even that had become insignificant in the face of recent events.

'Am I that fickle?' she asked fearfully. 'Is it possible to fall out of love with one man and into love with another so quickly?'

She laughed aloud, but there was no humour in it when she realised that it had taken falling in love with Matt to show her that she'd never really been in love before.

There was the sound of voices outside her door and she glanced up sharply, listening closely to find it was just some of the other guests.

A quick look at her watch told her that time had passed swiftly since she'd returned to her room and it was now nearly time to go and find a meal.

She glanced up at her reflection in the mirror and saw that she didn't look nearly as bad as she'd feared.

'A careful make-up job and I'd look almost present-able,' she decided. 'Can't skulk around here—not tonight. I'm going to push the boat out a bit so I'd better get moving.'

It was an hour before she was satisfied with her appearance, turning this way and that in front of the long mirror.

'Not bad,' she said with an approving nod. 'Even if I do say so myself.'

Everything she had on was new, from the ultra-sexy pure silk underwear in pale peach to the light-as-a-whisper honey-coloured silk dress that floated and skimmed around and over every curve and hollow like the most delicate of caresses. Slender-heeled strappy sandals made her feel tall and elegant and more than a match for whatever the future would bring.

'Here's to the first day of the rest of my life,' she said firmly, meeting her own gaze in the mirror with barely a quiver as she lifted her chin. 'Now all I need is my purse and my key.'

She'd barely been seated on one side of a table for four in a busy trattoria when a group of young English holidaymakers arrived, needing to push two tables together so that they could eat together. It was almost fate that hers was the only other nearby table free.

'Are you waiting for someone or would you like to join us?' their spokeswoman asked.

It took Lissa less than a second to decide that being part of such a lively group of women would be a far better way of pushing the boat out than doing it alone.

'I was on my own, but by all means let's push the tables together. The more the merrier.'

Over the course of a good-natured and sometimes noisy meal she learned that they were a group of uni-

versity students taking a cut-price last-minute break after a summer of paying off their first-year debts before
they embarked on the second year of their courses.

Lissa tried to remember if she'd ever been so light-
hearted about life, but there was too much noise to allow for serious thought.

Part way through their meal her neighbour nudged
her with an elbow to get her attention.

'Have you seen the local talent?' she murmured close
enough to Lissa's ear so that the comment was nearly
private. 'A whole group of them has just come in. Talk
about luck on our first evening here!'

Lissa glanced across and had to subdue a grimace
when she recognised some of the faces from the group
of predators she'd been seeing at intervals on the beach.

'Well, I hope you brought plenty of condoms with
you,' she said wryly, and wished she'd bitten her tongue
rather than make the comment when the others picked
up on it.

'Are they the local studs, then?' one asked eagerly.

'I've heard that about Italian lovers,' said another.
'Can they really keep it up all night?'

'I wouldn't know about that, and it wasn't what I
meant,' Lissa explained hurriedly, glad that the lighting
was low enough to hide the furious blush that was heating her cheeks. 'What I meant was that some of them
seem to pick up a different girl every week and sometimes every night, so if you didn't want to catch anything nasty it would be a good idea to take your own
precautions. You don't want a holiday fling to ruin the
rest of your life.'

Her mini-lecture definitely dampened their holiday
spirit and left Lissa feeling suddenly much more than
just a handful of years older than her companions.

It only took her a few minutes to decide that she was ready for her own company so she made her excuses and left to pay her bill, glimpsing movement out of the corner of her eye that told her the predators were on the prowl.

Well, she'd done her best to warn her temporary friends what the young men were like. It was up to the holidaymakers whether they were willing to run the risk.

She stood outside the trattoria for a moment trying to decide which way to go. It was just a short walk back to the hotel but she wasn't ready for the night to end just yet.

Unexpectedly, she found herself drawn towards the dark solitude of the beach.

So many memorable things had happened there in the short time since she'd arrived in San Vittorio, and now that she'd all but determined to return home as soon as a flight was available she wanted to make her farewells to the place without the company of noisy holidaymakers.

She didn't know how long she'd been standing in the lee of the rocks, staring out at the shifting sea, when she became aware of voices.

Her heart sank. The last thing she wanted was to be put in the uncomfortable position of an unwilling voyeur. If one of the young men had caught sight of fresh prey she hoped he wasn't intending coming any closer.

A group of shadows appeared between her and the sea and she stayed very still, hoping they would pass her by. She'd completely forgotten that the pale honey colour of her dress would show quite clearly against the darker rocks. It only took one person to spot her for the whole group to turn towards her.

'Hey, pretty lady. You are waiting for us?' called one in English. 'We saw you looking at us before you leave the trattoria so we follow.'

One of his companions made a crude suggestion in his own language and several laughed, obviously believing that she couldn't understand.

Her heart was beating like a trapped wild bird and she suddenly realised that she was in a far more precarious position than any of her erstwhile friends. At least they had the safety of numbers, while she had broken one of the cardinal rules of foreign travel.

'You are mistaken,' she said clearly, concentrating on sounding firm and in control. 'I am waiting for someone else. He should be arriving in a minute.'

'She's lying,' one sneered in his own tongue while another stuck to English.

'That's no problem. We can keep you company while you wait for him. Then, if he doesn't arrive, you've still got us.'

'I'm not waiting around,' grumbled another. 'Either I'm getting some from her or I'm off to find another one.'

'Don't be hasty,' advised the first voice. 'This one might be cool to start with but that sort usually warm up when they get going. Wait and see.'

The more Lissa heard the more frightened she became. She almost wished she hadn't known a single word of Italian rather than understand every degrading word.

She'd been enjoying the warm breeze but now she shivered, fear making her tremble.

She was all alone with no way of escaping and no weapon with which to defend herself except the pair of sandals clenched in one hand and the small purse tucked under her arm. She could try screaming, but there was no guarantee that anyone would hear her or that they would be able to pinpoint the direction before one of these predators silenced her.

All she had left was her wits, or what there was left of them.

'You're wrong,' she said firmly, reverting to Italian and thanking her grandmother for insisting on teaching her. 'I did not come here wanting your company. I want you to leave me alone.'

'And what if we don't want to leave you alone?' challenged a voice she hadn't heard before, obviously unimpressed by the fact that she could speak their language and had understood what they had in store for her.

'If you dishonour me then you will bring dishonour on your families,' she asserted, hoping that appealing to their strong belief in family honour would bring them to their senses. 'Is this what you would wish to happen to your sisters, your girlfriends?'

'They do not go onto the beach alone at night like you foreigners do. We know this is what you come away on holiday for.'

There was a hard edge to the voice that spoke those words, and when she saw them all begin to close in on her she realised that they were going to do what they'd come for no matter what she'd said.

All she could do now was fight as hard and as long as she could and hope to mark as many of them as possible. At least she would be able to pick them out by their injuries when she went to the police.

'Such pretty skin. So soft and smooth,' crooned one as he reached out to stroke her throat.

'Don't,' she snapped, knocking his hand away.

'Hey! You need to learn your place, woman,' another retorted. 'This is the South of Italy, not the North. Here the men are in charge, they way things are meant to be, and if we want to touch you…'

Hands moved swiftly, some reaching for her arms, another grabbing the top of her dress and jerking swiftly so that the neckline tore and gaped.

'No! Leave me alone!' she screamed, striking out with one high-heeled sandal and taking a savage delight in catching at least one tormentor. 'Don't touch me!'

There was a low concerted growl of anger at her defiance that made them seem even more like the predators she'd called them.

'Enough!' said one of the injured. 'She is only one and we are many. Grab her hands.'

They moved in on her again but before they could act they were distracted by the sound of swiftly moving feet pounding across the sand towards them.

'Get away from her!' roared an angry voice as Matt ploughed into them and sent them scattering and tumbling to the ground like so many skittles. 'You are worse than rabid animals.'

'Shh!' Matt soothed as he closed the door to Lissa's hotel room, his good arm wrapped securely around her shoulders. 'You're safe now, *cara*. The *carabinieri* caught every one of them before they could get off the beach.'

Lissa was trembling from head to foot as the scene she'd just endured played over in her head. For one dreadful moment she'd thought that there was no escape from what they intended…

She shuddered and shut the memory away, concentrating instead on the instant when Matt had done his heroic deed.

In response to her trembling he held her tighter, leading her across to the end of the closest bed where he helped her to sit.

She caught sight of the gaping front of her ruined dress and pulled his jacket closer around her to hide it. She felt safe now that she was with Matt but how had he known where she'd was and that she needed help?

'I didn't know you wore a big ''S'' on the front of your chest,' she tried to joke through chattering teeth. 'You certainly arrived in the nick of time, just like Superman.'

'It was more luck than super powers,' he admitted with an answering twinkle. 'I'd come here to invite you out for a meal but the receptionist told me you'd already gone out. He'd noticed which way you set off so I went looking.'

'You went looking for me?' she repeated in amazement as a warm glow began to permeate the chill inside.

'In every single restaurant until I met up with a group of English girls who seemed to know you. I don't know what you'd told them about me but I got a pretty frosty reception until I ''let slip'' that I'm a doctor you've been working with.'

'I hadn't spoken about you at all,' she reassured him hastily. And it certainly wouldn't have been in derogatory terms if she had, she added silently. 'I'd actually been warning them about those louts that cornered me. They were in the same trattoria, eyeing up the latest arrivals, and decided to follow me when I left.'

'Well, at that point I realised that you'd already eaten. I was on my way back here to pick up my car when I was sure I could hear your voice down on the beach.'

He paused and flicked her a glance that seemed almost uncomfortable. 'I wasn't certain whether you'd met someone and the two of you were...' He gestured awkwardly, still unaccustomed to having one hand out of action. 'Anyway, by the time you shouted at them I was only a hundred metres away and the rest...' He shrugged.

'But what on earth possessed you to charge at them like that?' she demanded, suddenly remembering that it hadn't been very long ago that she'd been stitching his hand. She reached out towards it. 'You could have ripped your stitches out and done permanent damage.'

'My hand's fine and I "charged", as you put it, because those louts were touching you against your will—hurting you. I couldn't let them do that to you.' There was steel in his voice and on his face and it brought back into vivid Technicolor the ferocious expression he'd worn when he'd taken on her attackers.

'Oh, God, Matt,' she moaned and covered her face. 'I should have known better than to walk down to the beach by myself. But it was such a lovely evening and it wasn't very late and...I wanted to be by myself for a while to do some thinking.' She drew in a shuddering breath and continued, needing to talk about what had happened. Perhaps that would take the edge off the remembered terror.

'I understood what they were saying but they had no idea I spoke Italian. I already knew the way they thought about young women holidaymakers because I've seen them and listened when they've been picking groups of girls up on the beach. Why I thought reasoning with them in their own language would work...' She shrugged helplessly. 'All it meant was that they took an extra delight in spelling out in detail what they were going to do to me.'

Lissa didn't know when the tears had started but her cheeks were wet.

'They made me feel dirty,' she whispered miserably. 'Not…not just where they touched me but…inside.'

'Shh,' Matt soothed, pulling her head down onto his shoulder and rocking her as gently as if she'd been a baby. 'Would a shower help you to feel clean again? Or a bath? I could run the water for you.'

The idea sounded blissful.

'Yes, please. A bath.' She grabbed for his arm when he went to stand up. 'You won't leave me?' she pleaded, hating to show such weakness but unable to help herself. 'I don't want to be here alone…not just yet.'

'Lissa, I'm not going anywhere,' he said firmly, giving her hand a reassuring squeeze. 'Maddelena is at home with Taddeo. She's staying the night so it doesn't matter how long you need me here.'

Matt wrapped his arm around her shoulder again as he helped her to her feet and guided her towards the bathroom.

It was easy enough to slip his jacket from her shoulders and hang it on the back of the door but it was a different matter when it came to undoing her dress.

For some reason the zip that had slid up so easily when she'd donned it a couple of hours ago was now out of reach, no matter how she contorted herself.

'Need some help?' he murmured and captured the offending tab and slid it smoothly to the bottom.

Thinking he was still involved in adjusting the temperature of the water, Lissa was taken completely by surprise as the silky fabric slithered towards the floor. She made a grab for it but it was too late.

'*Dio!*' Matt exclaimed angrily and she crossed her arms in front of herself, trying to hide the silky underwear that just seemed obscenely skimpy now. Embarrassment wouldn't let her look at his face and she couldn't imagine why he should be angry with her.

'Did they do this to you?' he demanded, his deep voice throbbing with pent-up emotion, and she was more confused than ever. 'If they hurt you…' His words faded into a silent threat as she glanced warily down at herself and saw the livid weals running diagonally from her collarbone to the very edge of her lacy bra.

She blinked in surprise as all became suddenly clear. 'I didn't know… It must have been when he grabbed my dress…'

Just saying the words brought the tremor back to her limbs. She was mesmerised as she watched Matt reach out to run one fingertip tenderly over each mark, and the trembling changed.

'Do they hurt?' he whispered but she barely heard him, fascinated to discover that his fingers were trembling, too.

'A little,' she admitted softly, then her breath caught in her throat when he bent to touch his lips to each mark.

'Kisses to make it better,' he explained with a hint of a smile as he straightened to his full height. 'Can you manage the rest?'

She glanced down at herself and only realised that he was teasing when she saw the front fastening on her bra.

'I think so,' she said, her mood lightening suddenly when she found herself fighting a grin of her own. He might be a caring doctor but the urge to flirt was obviously never far from the surface of his Italian soul. 'But I promise you'll be the first person I call if I need help.'

CHAPTER TEN

THE sound of the fishing boat engines drifted in through the open window as Lissa woke the next morning.

She smiled, certain she could pick out some of the voices calling out greetings as they approached the harbour wall.

This was such a nice way to wake up in the morning. So different from city traffic. Perhaps, when she went home, she would be able to find a job in one of the smaller regional hospitals.

She went to roll over on her back but there was something in her way—something large and warm and very masculine.

'Matt!' she breathed as everything that had happened the previous night came flooding back.

The ugly parts had even followed her into her dreams but, true to his promise, Matt had been there to reassure her that she wasn't alone and vulnerable.

Her heart swelled with gratitude and love for the gentle consideration he'd shown her. Why, it was almost as if he really cared for her, the way he'd settled her under the covers then curved himself protectively around her back.

She tried to turn to look at him but even in his sleep he tightened his arm to hold her safely in place.

Her heart gave an extra thump before she silently ordered it to behave.

Matt was a good and caring man and there had been more than one instance over the last weeks when he'd indicated that he was attracted to her, but he'd obviously been at great pains to explain to Taddeo why there was no chance of a permanent relationship between the two of them.

She sighed softly as resignation settled over her.

She'd come to Italy to get over the devastation of finding out that the man she'd been going to marry was a liar and a cheat. There was a small consolation in knowing that she'd discovered the truth about him before the wedding, but she'd honestly thought herself broken-hearted.

Until she'd met Matt and had got to know him. Now, even though she really knew what love was, it wasn't going to do her any good.

An ache settled heavily around her heart but she knew that she'd made the right decision last night. As soon as Matt left this morning, she was going to find out about an earlier flight back to England. There was no point in staying in San Vittorio any longer than she had to because the more she saw of him and his adorable son the more it would hurt to leave them.

Matt shifted behind her and she closed her eyes, cowardice prompting her to pretend she was still asleep. It was one thing to make a rational decision about leaving, but it would be another thing entirely to have to tell him face to face without breaking down in tears.

Perhaps she could leave a letter of explanation for him. At least that way she could choose her words and he wouldn't be able to see if she cried while she wrote them.

Stealthy movements behind her and the sound of fabric shifting against fabric told her that he was slipping away from her. Already, she felt lonely, missing the contact between their bodies even though they'd been separated all night by the bedclothes.

Concentrating on keeping her breathing steady, she followed the sounds as he retrieved his shoes and heard the soft jingle, swiftly muffled, as he picked up his keys.

It wasn't until she heard him release the lock on the door that she dared to open her eyes just far enough to take a last look at his departing figure.

'Goodbye, my love,' she breathed, tears already threatening as he gently pulled the door closed behind him and disappeared from her life for ever.

The scenery was so different to that around San Vittorio, Lissa thought as she followed the signs for Warminster.

Autumn was coming to England but everything here still looked so lush and green, where the Italian countryside had looked baked dry at the end of a summer of constant sun.

'Enough!' she exclaimed. 'That holiday was just three weeks out of your twenty-eight years. Get over it! There's the rest of your life to come.'

And, all of a sudden, the rest of her life seemed to be moving at a very rapid rate.

The travel company had found her a seat returning to England just five hours after she'd contacted them, and two days later she'd already had an interview for a job in Bristol. It was another city hospital, not the small regional hospital she'd been thinking about, but the accident and emergency department had recently been updated.

In the short time she'd been there it certainly seemed as if it would keep her busy enough not to leave too much time for remembering.

But she couldn't help thinking about the people and places she'd come to know.

She wondered if young Paolo had gained a little confidence now. It would have been nice to watch him develop into the excellent emergency physician that Matt was sure he'd eventually become. The number of staff at the Bristol hospital was so large that she'd probably never get to know any of them as well as she had the staff at San Vittorio, even in the few days she'd spent there.

She slowed down at the next set of signs, following the new direction for Longleat Wildlife Park.

Why she was doing this she didn't know, except while she'd been waiting for the time of her interview she'd seen an array of leaflets for local attractions. It had been pure chance that she'd glanced over the one for Longleat and had seen that the park was home to a pack of Canadian timber wolves. She hadn't been able to resist.

The wolves had their own enclosure within the park and it wasn't long before she was sitting quietly in the fading daylight, watching and waiting.

Almost as if he knew she wanted to see him, a heavily built male slipped silently out of the shadows of a group of trees and started to walk straight towards her. He was close enough for her to see the slightly green cast to his dark amber eyes when he halted.

Mesmerised, she stared at him, magnificent in his thickly furred majesty. His ears were pricked towards her almost as if he were listening to her thoughts, his eyes very intently watching.

Lissa could imagine only too easily how seeing such a creature at five years of age had made such a lasting impression on Matt. Had he kept his promise to Taddeo and taken him to see his surprise? Were the creatures he'd seen the same as this one?

She knew from the information sheet she'd been given that the Canadian timber wolf was a member of the same family as the grey wolf found in Italy's Abruzzi Mountains. Had Matt's wolf had the same dark mantle of fur over graduating shades of grey? Had the ears had a black line outlining their tips and had the belly fur been almost pure white?

How she wished she could have been there with the two of them when Matt told his son about that magical encounter with his grandfather. Having visited the place where it had happened, she felt almost as if she'd been there herself.

And it wasn't just that she wanted to be with them for the special occasions. She'd loved going on picnics with them and even on an ordinary visit to the beach. That wonderful home-cooked meal would have been nothing without the two of them there to eat it with her, and as for the bedtime ritual of reading a story...

It wasn't until she reached for her pocket in search of a hankie that she realised she was crying...again.

'This is stupid!' she exclaimed aloud then held her breath in case she'd startled her silent friend.

He seemed totally unworried by both her exclamation and her tears, still standing there as still and as silent as a statue with his eyes focused intently on her.

Suddenly she was struck by a strange sensation... almost as if he were trying to send her a message. Impossible, of course, but...the longer she stared into his eyes the calmer she became and the more certain that her life had taken a wrong turning.

'I don't belong in England any more,' she said softly

and a great weight dropped off her shoulders. 'I don't want that job in Bristol. I want to work in San Vittorio.'

She took a deep breath and straightened her shoulders with a new sense of purpose. Her trip to Italy had certainly had a potent effect on her, to say nothing of meeting the Aldarini men. It was time she did something about it.

'Perhaps there's a chance that Matt might learn to love me. If he doesn't, at least I will be able to work with him and see him and be a small part of his life.'

A niggling doubt tried to surface, accusing her of settling for just a shadow of a relationship rather than the real thing, but it didn't linger long.

Just staring into those strangely hypnotic eyes seemed to give her strength and determination.

Of course you want it all, said a voice inside her head. Give it a chance. It'll work out the way it's meant to.

Was it just wishful thinking or, like the faithful wolf, would she be lucky enough to have a lifetime with the mate she had chosen? Well, the only way she was ever going to find out was if she went back to San Vittorio.

'Thank you,' she whispered, even though she knew her watcher couldn't hear.

As if he knew that she didn't need him any more, the wolf suddenly turned and melted back into the growing shadows of the rapidly approaching evening.

'Time to go home,' she said as she reached for the keys then paused. 'No. Not home any more. San Vittorio is home now, with or without Matt and Taddeo in my life.'

There was a stranger's car in the space where Lissa usually parked and she was cursing softly as she had to reverse into an awkward spot.

Still it didn't dampen her spirits. She was going to be far too busy getting herself organised to worry about something as petty as a usurped parking space, even if it did mean she'd got to thread her way through the other cars carrying an awkward pile of empty cardboard boxes.

'First job, sort out the things I want to keep and get rid of the rest,' she muttered as the lift clanked and groaned its way up. 'There are several charity shops around who would welcome books and clothes.'

She'd have to sort out the legalities of terminating her lease. Would it be worth subletting for the rest of the year, or—?

Her train of thought was completely derailed when she turned the corner and walked full pelt into an immovable object. The pile of boxes tumbled in all directions, leaving her standing in their midst staring up into Matt's furious dark eyes.

'What is this nonsense?' he demanded, waving a crumpled fistful of paper in front of her face. 'You could not wait to speak to me and then I get *this*?'

Lissa gazed at him with her heart beating so fast and furiously that she couldn't have spoken even if she could have drawn enough breath.

She'd tried to blot out of her mind just how handsome he was, how tall and how broad his shoulders, and as for his accent... Hearing it so often while she'd been in San Vittorio, she'd almost forgotten how sexy it was until she heard it again in the prosaic surroundings of a drab apartment corridor.

'Well? Have you nothing to say?' he demanded impatiently.

Suddenly she felt like singing and dancing, like throwing her arms around him and holding on tight.

Matt was here! He was standing right in front of her with a thunderous scowl on his face, but he was *here*. That had to mean something, didn't it?

'Hello, Matt,' she said fighting a smile. Whatever happened in the next few minutes, it was *so* good to see him again, especially when she'd thought he was out of her life. 'Would you like to help me carry these into my flat?'

'No… Yes… *Why?* What are these for?' he demanded, sounding uncannily like his son.

He was confused, she realised, and her smile threatened to get completely out of control, the effect he had on her seeming stronger than ever.

'Because I've just called in at my local supermarket to collect them.'

'What for?' His hand was still bandaged, she noticed with relief, but he'd dispensed with the sling. He managed to stack several boxes inside each other and was trying to balance the rest on top one-handed.

'They're for packing,' she said, playing for time. This was a conversation she didn't really want to have in the corridor.

'Packing what?'

She unlocked her front door and swung it open for him to step inside.

'All my things.'

There was a sudden silence that wasn't solely due to him depositing his ungainly load. She leant back against the closed door waiting for him to ask why she needed to pack her belongings, but she should have known that he would have his own agenda.

'Where have you been all day?' he demanded, stepping closer to loom over her. 'I arrived here just after ten and you'd already gone out.'

'I had an interview in Bristol for a job in an accident and emergency department.' She straightened up and calmly walked past him into her tiny kitchen. She needed some coffee even if he would rather conduct an inquisition. Perhaps the smell of it would go some way towards mellowing his mood.

'And did you accept it?' he asked, his voice just inches behind her. He obviously wasn't letting her out of his sight until she told him what he wanted to know.

It did her heart good that he should automatically assume that she would have been offered the post.

'I told them I would let them know within forty-eight hours.'

The hospital hadn't been happy about that because they'd expected her to jump at such a big step up the career ladder, but even at that moment something had been telling her that she was going in the wrong direction.

She set the old-fashioned espresso-machine that had belonged to her Nonna to heat on the gas, and reached for two cups. She'd found her microwave was very good for heating a small amount of milk. She even had some powdered chocolate if he wanted some sprinkled on top, but, as ever, he'd probably prefer it black.

'And?' he prompted, asking for her decision. She intentionally took his question the wrong way.

'And then, on the way back here, I took a detour towards Warminster to visit Longleat Safari Park.'

'A safari park? Why, for heaven's sake?'

She turned to face him, deliberately looking him straight in the eye.

'Because they have a pack of wolves,' she said quietly, and watched him grow still.

'Wolves?' he repeated softly, a completely different expression in his voice and on his face. 'And why did you want to go and see the wolves?'

'Because…they made me think of you,' she admitted, taking her courage in both hands. He had done his part by travelling here from San Vittorio and she owed him nothing less than her honesty.

'And because I didn't get to see the wolves with you and Taddeo in the Abruzzi National Park,' she continued. 'But most of all…because I was missing you.'

'*Dio!*' he exclaimed, clearly exasperated. 'If you felt like that, why did you leave?'

The water in the espresso-machine started to boil but he reached out impatiently and turned it off before turning back to skewer her with his eyes.

Her courage nearly failed her but she realised that nothing would be gained by equivocation.

'Because I discovered I wanted more than you were prepared to offer,' she said quietly, terrified that such bluntness might lose her the chance of any sort of relationship with him. Unfortunately, knowing that she loved him meant that she would never be really happy with anything less than his love in return. Since meeting him, she'd come to realise that she couldn't accept half-measures.

'And did you ask *me* how I felt about it? What I was prepared to offer?' His voice mocked her choice of words even as he echoed them. 'No, you didn't. You just packed up your bags and disappeared. Can you imagine how upset Taddeo was when we arrived at the hotel that afternoon and found you'd gone? He blamed himself. He thought he must have done something to make you go away.'

'Oh, Matt, no. I'm so sorry!' She'd never dreamed that her little *girino* would take her departure that way.

'And then the receptionist handed me *that*!' He flung a disparaging hand at the crumpled letter now lying abandoned on the work surface. 'Full of platitudes that told me precisely nothing, so here I am to find out the real reason why you left so early.'

Lissa sighed silently.

Over the last two days she'd realised that she'd acted in a rude and cowardly way to have left like that, especially after Matt had rescued her from that group of over-sexed thugs and then stayed to soothe away her nightmares.

With hindsight she knew that it would have been far more adult of her to meet him just one more time to explain her reasons for going.

'This will take a little time,' she warned. 'And I'll need a cup of coffee because I haven't had anything to eat or drink since midday.'

Grudgingly, he stepped aside so that she could complete her preparations then followed her through into her sitting room.

Knowing how bland and utilitarian the colour scheme was in his little villa, she wasn't surprised when he stopped just inside the door and stared around him.

This was the room she had decorated with all the stories of Nonna's childhood in her mind. There was the ochre of the hillsides and the cerulean blue of the skies. There was deep turquoise and palest eau-de-nil for the Adriatic Sea and foliage plants of every shade green to reflect the stunning variety of trees and plants.

'So much colour!' he murmured as his eyes flew from

one place to another. 'So much life!' He stepped forwards to look closer at the photo that had pride of place on the mantelpiece.

'Your Nonna?' he asked with a raised eyebrow. 'You will look very much like her one day.'

'Thank you.' Lissa set the tray on the little coffee-table and sat on one end of the settee. After her insistence on making the coffee, she really couldn't face drinking it now.

'I decorated this room with all the colours she told me I'd find when I finally visited Italy,' she explained.

'And did you find them?' Matt lowered himself to the other end of the settee and she suddenly realised just how small it was. She could reach out her hand and touch him so easily...

'I found everything she'd always promised—blue sea and sky, white sand, rocks and plants of every shape. She warned me that the first time I visited it would have an effect on me that would never leave me. She also told me that Italian men were the most special in all the world. Fiercely proud and honourable but gentle and loving enough that you could safely trust a baby in their care.'

She looked up from the fingers laced together on her lap to meet his eyes.

'She also told me that they were the best lovers in the world, but...' She pressed her lips together and shook her head.

'You're not thinking about what happened to you on the beach. That's not—'

'No. I wasn't thinking about that,' she reassured him. 'I know there will always be bad apples in any barrel.'

'Then what?'

It was now or never.

'I left because I had found the man I could love for ever, but I didn't think he felt the same way about me.'

'*Finalmente!*' he exclaimed and leapt to his feet. 'At last we get there!'

He reached out to grab her hands and pulled her up into his arms.

'Woman, you must be mad! How could you *not* know that I fell in love with you the minute I saw you there taking care of my son as fiercely as if he were your own?'

With a harsh growl of frustration he pressed his lips to hers only to snatch them away again almost immediately.

'For nearly three weeks I have been trying to go slowly with you so I didn't frighten you away, but every time I thought we were making some progress you would look at me with pain and doubt in your eyes... Then those imbeciles on the beach dared to touch you...to hurt you.'

He gazed down at her. 'Tell me, honestly...truly. That was not why you went? Because of them? Because you did not feel safe?'

'Honestly, truly, it was for no other reason than because I had fallen in love with you.'

'Good,' he said decisively. 'A stupid reason to go, but good that you love me. Now you will be able to tell your Bristol hospital that you will not be taking their job because you will have one in San Vittorio.'

Lissa couldn't help chuckling.

'That was something else Nonna told me I would discover—the habit that Italian males have of ordering everybody about.'

'Well, you were going to pack up your things to go

to your new job, so why not bring them to San Vittorio with you instead?' he said with simple logic.

'Matt, I was going to pack my things up *because* I was going to come to San Vittorio. I'd already decided, when I was sitting looking at one of the wolves in the safari park, that I wanted to go back to Italy. That I'd left my heart with you and Taddeo.' A smile lifted the corners of her mouth and grew. 'Anyway, I still haven't found out whether Nonna told the truth about Italian men.'

'But you only need to know about this man,' he said with flattering possessiveness.

'Well, I know you're proud and stubborn and bossy and that you're a good and caring doctor and that you love your son.'

'So what else do you need to know?' There was that slightly arrogant tilt to his head that she had come to love.

She beckoned him closer with one finger until she could whisper in his ear.

'Why, Matt, I need to find out whether you're as good a lover as she promised.'

'Ah, my honey girl, I'm ready to prove it any time you want.'

'*Papà*, look!' Taddeo whispered, almost hoarse with excitement. 'It's a wolf! A real wolf!'

Matt was chuckling as he glanced across at Lissa. It had taken them several months to finally organise their postponed trip, but here they were in the Abruzzi National Park with one of the famous wolves trotting along the edge of the treeline.

It wasn't that they hadn't wanted to come sooner.

There had just been so many other things that had taken precedence.

Such as their wedding.

They'd intended to have a modest celebration, but once Justina had been told about their plans she wouldn't hear of it. In no time at all she'd seemed to have invited half of the population of San Vittorio, and had enlisted the aid of the other half to make it a truly memorable affair—no mean feat when she'd orchestrated the whole thing from a pair of crutches.

Still, they'd hardly been able to complain about her efforts when she'd also organised for Taddeo to join her extended family for a week to allow the newly-weds to have a proper honeymoon.

Then there had been the matter of paperwork to complete to ensure the approval of Lissa's appointment to the staff at San Vittorio Hospital.

It had been almost a foregone conclusion with her husband-to-be as one of her unofficial referees, but as she had already worked at the hospital on a voluntary basis when she'd first come to the town as a holiday-maker, the board was predisposed to like her.

As far as Taddeo was concerned, the best part about having Lissa as his new mother was that she'd actually let him help to choose the new colours they were painting their house, *and* let him help to do the painting.

Lissa knew that Matt loved the new life she'd brought to the villa and he'd told her more than once that she'd finally turned it into a home, but she knew that he was just grateful that the worst of it was over.

And now here they were to fulfil his promise.

'Is it a good surprise?' Lissa asked softly, glancing from one face to the other and seeing almost identical expressions of awe. It had been special for her to sit here holding Matt's hand while he'd told Taddeo about his long-ago vigil with his grandfather.

'It's a *perfect* surprise,' Taddeo corrected.

'Look, *caro*,' Matt said and pointed a little farther off.

'There's more of them!' the youngster exclaimed, barely remembering to keep his voice low. 'Some of them are smaller than the others.'

'That's probably the mother wolf with her cubs,' Matt explained. 'They were probably born around the time you were eating your Easter egg.'

Lissa was waiting for the questioning glance he sent her way and gave her head a slight shake.

'Not yet,' she murmured softly, resting her head on his shoulder to keep their conversation private from Taddeo. He was probably far too enraptured with what was going on outside the car to bother listening, but still she was careful.

'Nine months' wait seems long enough to us. To him it will stretch out for ever.'

He nodded his agreement and bent to brush a kiss over her lips.

'So tell me, Dr Aldarini, have you come to any conclusions about what your Nonna promised?' he demanded with laughter in his husky murmur.

'Her promise?' As ever, his kiss distracted her so much she could hardly think straight, but she couldn't resist the urge to tease. 'That visiting Italy would have a permanent effect on my life?'

'That Italian men make the best lovers, of course,' he contradicted in a voice husky enough to make her think about tumbled sheets and warm caresses.

'Ah, that promise!' She chuckled. 'Well, Dr Aldarini, you were sexy enough to make me pregnant on my honeymoon but as to *that* promise, I couldn't possibly say—otherwise you might stop trying to prove it.'

Modern Romance™
...seduction and
passion guaranteed

Tender Romance™
...love affairs that
last a lifetime

Sensual Romance™
...sassy, sexy and
seductive

Blaze™
...sultry days and
steamy nights

Medical Romance™
...medical drama on
the pulse

Historical Romance™
...rich, vivid and
passionate

29 new titles every month.

With all kinds of Romance for
every kind of mood...

MILLS & BOON®

Makes any time special™

MAT4

books and a surprise gift!

We would like to take this opportunity to thank you for reading this Mills & Boon® book by offering you the chance to take FOUR more specially selected titles from the Medical Romance™ series absolutely FREE! We're also making this offer to introduce you to the benefits of the Reader Service™—

- ★ FREE home delivery
- ★ FREE gifts and competitions
- ★ FREE monthly Newsletter
- ★ Exclusive Reader Service discounts
- ★ Books available before they're in the shops

Accepting these FREE books and gift places you under no obligation to buy, you may cancel at any time, even after receiving your free shipment. Simply complete your details below and return the entire page to the address below. *You don't even need a stamp!*

YES! Please send me 4 free Medical Romance books and a surprise gift. I understand that unless you hear from me, I will receive 6 superb new titles every month for just £2.49 each, postage and packing free. I am under no obligation to purchase any books and may cancel my subscription at any time. The free books and gift will be mine to keep in any case.

M1ZEA

Ms/Mrs/Miss/Mr ....Initials.......................................
                                                    BLOCK CAPITALS PLEASE
Surname ....
Address ....
....
....Postcode...................................

Send this whole page to:
UK: FREEPOST CN81, Croydon, CR9 3WZ
EIRE: PO Box 4546, Kilcock, County Kildare (stamp required)

Offer valid in UK and Eire only and not available to current Reader Service subscribers to this series. We reserve the right to refuse an application and applicants must be aged 18 years or over. Only one application per household. Terms and prices subject to change without notice. Offer expires 30th April 2002. As a result of this application, you may receive offers from other carefully selected companies. If you would prefer not to share in this opportunity please write to The Data Manager at the address above.

Mills & Boon® is a registered trademark owned by Harlequin Mills & Boon Limited.
Medical Romance™ is being used as a trademark.